BAD SEED

BY MAXWELL ANDERSON

**THE DRAMATIZATION OF
WILLIAM MARCH'S NOVEL
*THE BAD SEED***

DRAMATISTS
PLAY SERVICE
INC.

BAD SEED was first presented in New York City on December 8, 1954, at the Forty-sixth Street Theater. It was directed by Reginald Denham, and the setting and lighting were by George Jenkins. The cast was as follows:

RHODA PENMARK ....Patty McCormack
COL. KENNETH PENMARK ....John O'Hare
CHRISTINE PENMARK ....Nancy Kelly
MONICA BREEDLOVE ....Evelyn Varden
EMERY WAGES ....Joseph Holland
LEROY ....Henry Jones
MISS FERN ....Joan Croydon
REGINALD TASKER ....Lloyd Gough
MRS. DAIGLE ....Eileen Heckart
MR. DAIGLE ....Wells Richardson
MESSENGER ....George Gino
RICHARD BRAVO ....Thomas Chalmers

SCENE

The apartment of Col. and Mrs. Penmark, in the suburb of a Southern city.

ACT I

SCENE 1: Early morning. A day in early June.
SCENE 2: 2:30 P.M., the same day.
SCENE 3: Evening, the same day.
SCENE 4: Mid-morning, a few days later.

ACT II

SCENE 1: Late afternoon, the next day.
SCENE 2: After breakfast, the next morning.
SCENE 3: After dinner, the same day.
SCENE 4: A few days later.

BAD SEED

ACT I

SCENE 1

The one set is the apartment of Colonel and Mrs. Penmark, in a small town in a southern state. We see a tastefully furnished room with colonial pieces and reproductions, expensive but not too gaudy. At R. is an arch door surrounded by bookcases with cupboards at the bottom of each side. A mirror is above one of the shelves of the D. S. bookcase. This door leads off to an inner hall and the bedrooms. At R. rear is the door to the kitchen which is partially visible. The stove can be seen. A large bay window with a window seat is at C. rear. Heavy drapes which cover the window area are open and the room is flooded with early morning light. A small toy dog is L. on the seat. There is a platform extending from the U. L. corner to the D. L. corner of the set giving a sunken living room effect. The door to the den, containing a piano, is at L. rear on this platform as is the front door at L. There is a small table with a drawer, D. R. under the bookcases. Rhoda Penmark, their daughter, keeps her "treasures" in the drawer and it is generally understood that this is her table. An ashtray is on the table. The U. S. cupboard under the bookcase contains Rhoda's things too—shoes, skates, etc. There is a large armchair D. R. with a small table above and L. of it. A spice cabinet hangs on the wall R. of the kitchen door. A chest of drawers to the L. of the kitchen door with a lamp on it. A dining table is up in the bay window with matching dining chairs R. and L. A sofa at L. with a coffee table below it and a stool to the R. On the coffee table are an ashtray and matches. Another armchair is down L. of the sofa. Kenneth's hat is on it. Between the

*front and den doors on the platform is a desk, with a
lamp and telephone, and a desk chair. A small radio is
on a shelf above the desk and a waste basket is D. S. of
the desk. There is a large chandelier hanging from the
ceiling in the C. of the room and a smaller one hanging
near the front door which serve as general lighting at
night.*

*Rhoda Penmark, a neat, quaint and pretty little girl of
eight, sits seriously reading a book on the chair R. She
wears a red and white dotted Swiss dress and red shoes
with metal pieces on the heels. She turns a page carefully, absorbed in the story. Colonel Kenneth Penmark,
a good looking officer of thirty-five or so, comes in from
R., carrying two fairly new suitcases.*

KENNETH. (*Entering.*) Why, 'morning, Rhoda!

RHODA. 'Morning, Daddy.

KENNETH. (L. *of chair.*) Up and dressed and ready for the day!
Wearing your best perfume?

RHODA. (*Marking her place.*) Yes, I am, Daddy.

KENNETH. (*Crossing R. to door.*) That's right, this is the day
of the picnic. I hope there's a breeze off the water. (*He sets bags
on floor D. S. of front door.*)

RHODA. Miss Fern says there always is.

KENNETH. (*Crossing to Rhoda, examining plane ticket which
he takes from breast pocket.*) She says it never rains on the first
of June, too. Don't count on it.

RHODA. Are you leaving today, Daddy?

KENNETH. (*Stops L. of Rhoda.*) My plane goes in an hour.
Back to Washington and the Pentagon and a climate that coddles
eggs.

RHODA. I like coddled eggs.

KENNETH. You like everything. You're just too good to be true.
(*He pulls her braids, and she smiles up at him.*)

RHODA. How long will you be gone? (*Puts her book on chair.*)

KENNETH. (*Turns away from Rhoda, looking at watch.*) Sealed
orders, darling. All I know is I'll be home as soon as I can. (*He
turns and kneels and holds out his arms to Rhoda.*) Now what will
you give me if I give you a basket of kisses?

6

RHODA. (*Rises.*) I'll give you a basket of hugs. (*Rhoda jumps into father's arms and hugs him.*)

KENNETH. (*He stands holding her in his arms.*) I like your hugs.

RHODA. I like your kisses. Daddikins! You're so big and strong!

KENNETH. I'll miss you. The general doesn't have one pretty girl on his whole staff!

RHODA. I wish he didn't have my daddy! I'll miss you every day!

KENNETH. Will you write to me? (*Puts her down.*)

RHODA. Do you want me to?

KENNETH. Of course I want you to.

RHODA. Then I'll write to you every day.

KENNETH. Every time I write to Mother I'll put in a note for you!

RHODA. Will you really?

KENNETH. Really and truly. And every time the general tells a good joke I'll send you an official report!

RHODA. Oh, Daddy, that won't be very often! You'd better send me the bad ones too!

KENNETH. (*Kisses top of her head.*) Sweetheart, I will! (*Mrs. Penmark comes in from the den* U. L. *She is somewhat under thirty, a very pretty, gentle and gracious woman, quite obviously dedicated to her husband and child. The kind of woman whose life is given meaning by the affection she gives and receives. Kenneth kisses Christine, his wife, who has brought his briefcase and she goes into his arms without a word. They have said good-bye previously, but she can't let him go without another embrace.*) I shall write daily to both my sweethearts, unless somebody makes a mistake and starts a shooting war and we all have to go underground.

RHODA. (*Seated in chair* R.) Would you go underground if there was a war?

KENNETH. (*To Rhoda.*) Yes, I would, and, by gum, I'd go fast!

RHODA. You said "by gum" because I was here.

KENNETH. That's right, I did.

CHRISTINE. (*To Kenneth.*) Darling, take care.

KENNETH. (*To Christine.*) I will. Every minute I'm away. I'll wire you the minute we're on the ground. Take care of each other, you two.

CHRISTINE. We will. (*The doorbell* L. *rings a delicate little*

7

chime.) That's Monica and Emory. They wanted to say a last good-bye to you.

KENNETH. Oh, sure. (*He crosses above Christine to the front door and puts briefcase on chair* D. L. *Meanwhile Christine crosses behind chair* R., *looks at Rhoda's hair and as she touches her braid Rhoda draws away*.)

RHODA. Is it all right?

CHRISTINE. It's perfect, darling, braids and all. (*Turns to welcome Monica and Emory*.)

KENNETH. (*At the front door* L.) Come in, Monica. Come in, Emory. (*Mrs. Monica Breedlove is a widow of forty-five or so, plump, intelligent, voluble and perhaps over-friendly. She carries sunglasses with a case and a locket in her hand. Her brother, Emory Wages, is a few years younger than she, also plump and friendly, but in contrast almost taciturn*.)

MONICA. (*Crosses behind sofa to Christine*.) Just the effusive neighbors from upstairs, darlings! Have to be in on everything. No lives of their own, so they live other people's. I speak for my brother as well as myself, because he never gets a chance to speak when I'm around. (*Turns to Kenneth*.) There, I've talked enough. Say something, Colonel.

KENNETH. (*Behind sofa*.) I guess it will have to be good-bye, because the taxi's here and I don't want to rush through traffic.

EMORY. (*At door*.) Don't worry about your two pretty girls, Ken. We'll keep an eye on them, and if one of them begins to look peaked, we'll send up smoke signals.

KENNETH. I'm counting on you, Emory. (*He gives Monica his hand*.) And on Monica.

MONICA. Good-bye, Kenneth.

KENNETH. (*Crosses to Christine*.) Well, sweetheart, this is it. (*To Rhoda*.) Good-bye, big eyes!

RHODA. (*Seated chair* R.) Good-bye, Daddy.

CHRISTINE. (*They cross hand in hand below coffee table to front door*.) I promised myself I wouldn't come down, but ——

KENNETH. Don't, sweet. It's just another empty month or two. We'll get through them somehow. (*He picks up his hat and briefcase*.)

EMORY. I'll take those. (*He precedes Kenneth out of front door with both of the bags. Kenneth and Christine embrace*.)

KENNETH. Good-bye. (*He exits* L.)

8

MONICA. Poor boy. He hates to go. And you hate to let him go. (*Christine is still looking out the door.*)

CHRISTINE. I'm—not very self-sufficient. (*She shuts door.*)

MONICA. Well, I am, and it's not so good. You're in love, both of you, you lucky characters. I wish I were. (*Looks toward Rhoda, then back to Christine.*) Oh, by the way, nobody has to take Rhoda to the bus, because I made some cupcakes for Miss Fern, and she's coming by to pick them up.

CHRISTINE. Oh, good. (*Crosses to sofa.*)

MONICA. (*To Rhoda, crossing D. C.*) But before she comes I have two little presents for you, my darling.

RHODA. (*Rises, crosses C. to Monica. Christine sits L. end sofa.*) Presents!

MONICA. The first is from Emory. It's a pair of dark glasses with rhinestone decorations, and he said to tell you they're intended to keep the sun out of those pretty blue eyes. (*She produces the glasses, and Rhoda goes toward her with an eager expression which her mother knows as Rhoda's "acquisitive look."*) I'll try them on you. (*Rhoda stands obediently while Monica adjusts the glasses. To Christine.*) Now who is this glamorous Hollywood actress? Can it really be little Rhoda Penmark who lives with her delightful parents on the first floor of my apartment house?

RHODA. (*Crosses to mirror on D. S. shelf bookcase and looks at her reflection in the glass.*) I like them. (*Crosses back to Monica.*) Where's the case?

MONICA. Here it is. (*Hands case to Rhoda.*) And now for the second present, which is from me. (*She holds up a little gold heart with a chain attached.*) This was given to me when I was eight years old, (*To Christine.*) it's a little young for me now, (*To Rhoda.*) but it's still just right for an eight-year-old. However, it has a garnet set in it, and we'll have to change that for a turquoise since turquoise is your birthstone. So I'll have it changed and cleaned, and then it's yours.

RHODA. (*To Monica.*) Could I have both stones? The garnet, too?

CHRISTINE. Rhoda! Rhoda! What a ——

MONICA. (*Laughing turns to Christine.*) But of course, she may! Why, certainly! How wonderful to meet such a natural little girl! She knows what she wants and she asks for it—not like these over-civilized little pets that have to go through analysis before they can choose an ice cream soda! (*Rhoda goes to her, puts her arms around her waist and hugs her with an intensity which gives Monica great delight.*)

RHODA. (*Purring.*) Aunt Monica! Dear, sweet Aunt Monica! (*Monica is completely captivated, but Christine looks on with a slightly skeptical and concerned attitude. She knows that Rhoda is not really affectionate, that she is acting. She rises, crosses to desk and sits writing on pad.*)

MONICA. I know I'm behind the times, but I thought children wore coveralls and play-suits to picnics. Now you, my love, look like a princess in that red and white dotted Swiss. Tell me, aren't you afraid you'll get it dirty? Or you'll fall and scuff those new shoes? (*Rhoda shakes her head slowly "Uh, uh."*)

CHRISTINE. (*Looking toward Monica and Rhoda.*) She won't soil the dress and she won't scuff the shoes. Rhoda never gets anything dirty, though how she manages it, I don't know.

RHODA. I don't like coveralls. They're not— (*She hesitates.*)

MONICA. You mean coveralls aren't quite ladylike, don't you, my darling? (*She embraces the tolerant Rhoda again.*) Oh, you old-fashioned little dear!

RHODA. (*Looking at the locket.*) Am I to keep this now?

MONICA. You're to keep it till I find out where I can get the stone changed.

RHODA. Then I'll put it in my box. (*She goes to her table, opens the drawer and a box which once held Swiss chocolates and places the locket carefully inside. A voice says "Leroy" as the front door L. swings open. The house-man, or janitor, stands in the doorway. He carries a pail, sponge and equipment for washing windows.*)

LEROY. (*The janitor crossing R. behind sofa.*) Leroy. Guess I'm pretty early, Mrs. Penmark, but it's my day for doing the windows on this side.

CHRISTINE. Oh, yes, you can begin in the bedroom, Leroy. (*He crosses C. and rather than going around Monica comes behind her.*)

LEROY. (*To Monica.*) Excuse me, ma'am. (*Monica is startled, exchanges a look with Christine as she crosses and sits R. end of the sofa. To Rhoda.*) Mornin'. (*Crosses through the inner hall with pail and paraphernalia. Rhoda skips across room and sits on stool.*)

RHODA. I like garnets, but I like turquoise better.

MONICA. (*To Rhoda.*) You sound like Fred Astaire, tap-tapping across the room. What have you got on your shoes?

RHODA. (*Shows bottom of shoe to Monica.*) I run over my heels, and Mother had these iron pieces put on so they'd last longer.

CHRISTINE. (*At desk.*) I'm afraid I can't take any credit. It was Rhoda's idea entirely.

RHODA. I think they're very nice. They save money.

MONICA. Oh, you penurious little sweetheart! But I'll tell you one thing, Rhoda, I think you worry too much when you're not the very best at everything. That's one reason Emory and I thought you should have some presents today. You wanted that penmanship medal very much, didn't you?

RHODA. It's the only gold medal Miss Fern gives. And it was really mine. Everybody knew I wrote the best hand and I should have had it. (*Leroy comes from off* R. *toward the kitchen with his pail and sponge.*)

LEROY. 'Scuse me, just gettin' some water. (*He goes to the kitchen.*)

RHODA. I just don't see why Claude Daigle got the medal.

CHRISTINE. (*Rises, crosses behind sofa to Rhoda.*) Rhoda, these things happen to us all the time, and when they do we simply accept them. I've told you to forget the whole thing. (*She puts an arm around Rhoda, trying to soften her. Rhoda rises, pulls away impatiently.*) I'm sorry. I know you don't like people pawing over you.

RHODA. (*She stamps away to chair* R.) It was mine! The medal was mine!

CHRISTINE. (*Christine follows, trying to soothe her.*) Rhoda, forget it. Put it out of your mind.

RHODA. (*She stamps away again to her table.*) I won't. I won't. I won't. (*Leroy comes out of the kitchen with the pail, passes near Rhoda, and squeezing his sponge, spills water on her new shoes.*)

MONICA. (*Rises.*) Leroy! Have you completely lost your senses? You spilled water on Rhoda's shoes!

LEROY. (*Crosses toward Christine.*) I'm sorry, ma'am. I guess I was just trying to hurry. (*He turns and deliberately drops his sponge on Christine's dress. She crosses to stool and sits.*)

11

MONICA. Leroy!

LEROY. (L. *of chair.*) I'm sorry, Mis' Breedlove. (*Kneels, facing upstage.*)

MONICA. Leroy, I own this apartment house! I employ you! (*Crosses to Leroy, standing over him.*) I've tried to give you the benefit of every doubt because you have a family! I've thought of you as emotionally immature, torn by irrational rages, a bit on the psychopathic side. But after this demonstration I think my diagnosis was entirely too mild. You're definitely a schizophrenic with paranoid overtones. (*He turns downstage.*) I've had quite enough of your discourtesy and surliness—and so have the tenants in the building! (*Crosses to Christine.*) My brother Emory has wanted to discharge you! I've been on your side, though with misgivings! I shall protect you no longer!

CHRISTINE. (*Touching Monica's arm.*) He didn't mean it, Monica. It was an accident. I'm sure it was.

RHODA. (*Crosses to Leroy—stares into his face.*) He meant to do it. I know Leroy well.

MONICA. It was no accident, Christine! It was deliberate—the spiteful act of a neurotic child.

RHODA. (*Crosses to Leroy.*) He meant to do it. (*To Leroy.*) You made up your mind to do it when you went through the room.

CHRISTINE. (*Trying to avoid embarrassing Leroy.*) Rhoda!

RHODA. I was looking at you when you made up your mind to wet us.

LEROY. Oh, I never, I never, I'm just clumsy. (*He takes sponge and wipes Rhoda's shoes.*)

CHRISTINE. (*Stands impatiently, crosses to sofa.*) Oh, Leroy, please, please! (*Rhoda draws away.*)

MONICA. My patience is at an end, and you may as well know it. (*Leroy gets up.*) Go about your work.

LEROY. Yes, ma'am. (*He exits into hall, taking pail and sponge with him.*)

MONICA. (*As Leroy disappears.*) He has the mind of an eight-year-old, but he has managed to produce a family so I keep him on. (*The doorbell chimes.*) That'll be Miss Fern. (*Crosses to R. end sofa.*)

CHRISTINE. (*Crosses below sofa to front door.*) Yes. Come in, Miss Fern. We're nearly ready, I think.

MISS FERN. (*At front door.*) I'm a bit ahead of time, as usual.

12

(*She comes in primly, coming down* R. *of* L. *chair. As the head of the most aristocratic school in the state, she has achieved a certain savoir faire, though she is in herself a timid and undistinguished little old maid, making the most of the remains of once quite remarkable beauty.*)

MONICA. (*Back to sofa.*) Oh, Miss Fern, the old scatterbrain left her two dozen cupcakes upstairs. Rhoda, will you help me carry them down?

RHODA. (*Crossing to* C.) Yes, of course I will.

MONICA. (*Crossing to front door and waits at door for Rhoda.*) They're all packed.

RHODA. (*At* C. *stage, she curtsies to Miss Fern.*) Good morning, Miss Fern.

MISS FERN. (*Crosses below sofa to* R. *end of sofa.*) That's a perfect curtsey, Rhoda.

RHODA. Thank you, Miss Fern. (*She crosses below coffee table and exits with Monica through front door.*)

CHRISTINE. She does such things well? (*Closes door, crosses to sofa.*)

MISS FERN. She does everything well. As you must know better than I.

CHRISTINE. And, as a person, does she fit in well—at the school?

MISS FERN. Let me think—(*She sits* R. *end of sofa.*) in what way, Mrs. Penmark?

CHRISTINE. (*At* L. *end of sofa.*) Well, Rhoda has been—I don't quite know how to say it. There's a mature quality about her that's disturbing in a child. My husband and I thought that a school like yours, where you believe in discipline and the old-fashioned virtues—might perhaps teach her to be a bit more of a child.

MISS FERN. Yes—yes, I know what you mean. In some ways, in many ways, Rhoda is the most satisfactory pupil the school has ever had. She's never been absent. She's never been tardy. She's the only child in the history of the school who has made a hundred in deportment each month in every class, and a hundred in self-reliance and conservation on the playground each month for a full school year. If you had dealt with as many children as I have, you'd realize what a remarkable record that is. And she's the neatest little girl I've ever encountered.

13

CHRISTINE. (*Sits on* L. *arm of sofa.*) Kenneth says he doesn't know where she gets her tidiness. Certainly not from him or me.

MISS FERN. And she has many good qualities. She's certainly no tattletale.

CHRISTINE. Oh?

MISS FERN. One of our children broke a window across the street and we knew that Rhoda knew who it was. When we questioned her about it, and told her it was her duty as an honorable citizen to report the offender, she just went on eating her apple, shaking her head, denying that she knew anything about it—and looking us over with that pitying, calculating look she has at certain times.

CHRISTINE. Oh, I know that look so well!

MISS FERN. But that was admirable too for she was merely being loyal to a playmate.

CHRISTINE. Then—do the other children like her? Is she popular?

MISS FERN. The other children. Well, I —— (*Miss Fern hesitates, trying to think of something to say, and is saved from having to answer by the re-entry at front door of Monica and Rhoda, carrying two small packed baskets.*)

MONICA. Here we are!

MISS FERN. (*Rises.*) Then I suppose we should go, for my sisters and the others will be waiting. Good-bye, Mrs. Penmark.

CHRISTINE. (*Crosses to Miss Fern and shakes hand. And Miss Fern crosses up around* R. *end of sofa.*) Good-bye! May it be everything a picnic should be!

MISS FERN. Thank you. Come, Rhoda.

RHODA. Yes, Miss Fern. (*She crosses in front of sofa to be kissed by her mother.*)

MONICA. (*At* U. S. *door.*) Calm sea and prosperous voyage!

MISS FERN. (*Crosses to front door, takes one basket from Monica, stands* L. *of Monica waiting for Rhoda.*) Thank you! We'll take care of her! (*Rhoda runs to Monica for a last quick hug.*) No time! We're off!

MONICA. (*Gives Rhoda a hug.*) We stole time, didn't we, Rhoda?

MISS FERN. Bless you both! (*She goes out front door with Rhoda.*)

MONICA. (*Closing front door and crossing* C.) So now the older

16

set's left behind with nothing to do. (*Christine takes Rhoda's book from chair R. and puts it on D. R. table and sits in chair R.*)

CHRISTINE. I suppose I could go through the dreary business of trying to make my face presentable. It happens every morning.

MONICA. (*Up to L. of Christine.*) Your face! Think of mine!

CHRISTINE. It always makes me gloomy when Kenneth goes away. Anything could happen—before I see him again. There's an old saying—we die a little at parting.

MONICA. My dear, we die a little every day if we want to brood about it! (*Crosses to Christine.*) Why don't we make some kind of party of this? You're having Emory and Reginald Tasker to lunch—can't I help with that?

CHRISTINE. What do you feed a criminologist?

MONICA. Oh, prussic acid, blue vitriol, ground glass ——

CHRISTINE. Oh, hot weather things!

MONICA. (*Laughs.*) Nothing would hurt Reggie. He thrives on buckets of blood and sudden death.

CHRISTINE. How many mysteries has he written?

MONICA. A complete set of his works would encircle the Empire State building—or me. Come on—(*Takes her by the hand and Christine rises.*) I'm a garrulous old hag, but I can grind glass. We're not going to let you be lonely. (*They go into the kitchen, Christine preceding, and close the door. Leroy comes in from hall R. carrying pail and newspaper. Crosses to kitchen door. Listens —then crosses to dining table.*)

LEROY. That know-it-all, Monica Breedlove, she don't think nobody knows anything but her. (*Sets pail on floor R. of table.*) I'll show that bitch plenty. (*Spreads newspaper on table.*) And that young trough-fed Mrs. Penmark. (*Sets pail on table.*) She don't get enough of what she needs; I could give it to her. (*Picks up small toy dog from window seat L.*) Rhoda now. That's a smart little girl. She's almost as smart as I am. She sees through me and I see through her. By damn she's smart. (*Pulls curtain open and closes window as curtain falls.*)

CURTAIN

15

ACT I

SCENE 2

It is 2:30 p.m. the same day. Christine has served lunch in her apartment to Emory Wages (seated chair L. of table) and his sister Monica (seated c. window seat), also to Reginald Tasker (seated R. of Monica on window seat), a friend of theirs who writes detective stories and has made himself a minor expert in the history of crime. The luncheon dishes have mostly been removed, and the guests still linger over their iced tea, cheese and fruit. The men have taken off their coats, Tasker's is on window seat, and Emory's is on back of D. L. chair. As curtain goes up—Tasker and Emory are laughing as Christine enters from kitchen with pitcher of iced tea, which she puts on coffee table.

MONICA. (*To Christine.*) But I did meet him. Nobody ever believes me when I tell them I met Sigmund Freud —— (*Christine sits in chair R. of table.*)

EMORY. Come now—they believe you ——

MONICA. You mean it's automatic flattery. They know I'm old enough, but they voice doubts to make me feel better —— Well, anyway, it wasn't Dr. Freud who analyzed me, it was Dr. Kettlebaum in London.

EMORY. (*Eating grapes.*) Now we're off.

MONICA. And this was my choice, too. Not that I minimize Freud's professional standing, for I still consider him the great genius of our time—but Dr. Kettlebaum was more—more simpatico, if you know what I mean, Reggie.

EMORY. (*To Tasker.*) It means simpatico if you know what that means.

MONICA. Freud loathed American women.

CHRISTINE. Oh?

MONICA. Especially the ones that talked back to him, and I

16

loathed his Germanic prejudice against feminine independence, which he couldn't conceal.

CHRISTINE. Was Freud prejudiced?

MONICA. Indeed he was. Not consciously, you know. He just bristled when I suggested that women had more sense than men. Now Dr. Kettlebaum believed in the power of the individual soul, and considered sex of only trivial interest. His mind was less literal, more mystic, like my own.

CHRISTINE. (*Eating bit of cheese.*) Oh, Monica, really! Did the analysis do you any good, actually?

MONICA. Well, it broke up my marriage. (*Christine and Tasker laugh.*) I looked into the very bottom of my soul. What a spectacle! When I came back I asked Mr. Breedlove for a divorce and he didn't oppose it. So then I decided that what I'd always really wanted was to make a home for my brother—and so I did. I don't think dear Emory appreciates it, but what woman ——

EMORY. (*Tired of hearing the story for the hundredth time.*) I can stand anything except talk about your analysis—and analyzing of your friends—and me. I don't want to look into the bottom of my soul.

MONICA. (*To Emory.*) I can understand that perfectly. (*To Christine and Tasker.*) We're all so sensitive about these things. The truth absolutely disgusts us. Now I've come to the conclusion that Emory is a "larvated homosexual" ——

CHRISTINE. (*Christine chokes on her iced tea.*) Whaaat!

EMORY. (*Exploding.*) Thank you. What does larvated mean?

MONICA. It means covered as with a masque—concealed.

TASKER. It means something that hasn't come to the surface—as yet.

EMORY. (*Leaning back in chair.*) You can say that again. If I'm a homosexual, they'll have to change the whole concept of what goes on among 'em.

TASKER. Where do you get that idea, Monica?

MONICA. Pure association, the best evidence of all. Emory's fifty-two years old, and he's never married. I doubt if he's ever had a serious love affair.

EMORY. (*Defending himself.*) How would you know if they're serious?

MONICA. Please, let's look at things objectively. (*Emory rises impatiently, crosses L. to U. L. of sofa and takes cigar from shirt*

17

pocket.) What are Emory's deepest interests in life? They are—fishing, murder mysteries in which housewives are dismembered, canasta, baseball games, and singing in male quartets. How does Emory spend Sundays? He spends them on a boat with Reggie and other men—fishing. And are there ladies present on these occasions? There are not.

EMORY. (*Cutting end of cigar.*) You're damned right there are not!

MONICA. I guess you are all shocked, aren't you? But you shouldn't be. Actually, homosexuality is triter than incest. (*Christine and Tasker exchange a glance.*) Dr. Kettlebaum considered it was all a matter of personal preference. Now I'm perfectly frank about myself. (*To Emory.*) Subconsciously I have an incestuous fixation on Emory. (*To Christine.*) It's not normal, but that's the way it is.

EMORY. (*At L. end of sofa.*) Thanks a million, little sister. (*Throwing up his hands.*) Can't we talk about something normal, like murder? Anybody mind if I smoke a cigar? (*He turns and starts down L. to D. L. chair.*)

MONICA. What are you trying to prove, Emory? (*Emory stopped by this remark, turns to answer—but decides it's useless. He continues down to D. L. chair and takes matches from his coat which hangs on the back and sits.*)

CHRISTINE. (*Rises, takes tea and glass, crosses to sofa, sits at R. end.*) Let's relax away from the table and have our tea over here.

MONICA. (*Rises, crosses L. back of sofa, hands her glass to Christine and continues around sofa.*) Yes, we've run through sex. Let's try homicide. Reggie, you're the expert. (*Points to Tasker who has risen and crossing D. R.*)

EMORY. (*Seated in D. L. chair.*) Any change is for the better.

TASKER. (*At table near D. R. chair, taking cigarette.*) All right, I'll oblige. I've been collecting data on Mrs. Allison lately. (*Monica sits at L. end sofa as Christine hands her glass of tea.*) *News Budget* wants an article on her, but I can't say she's a very flaming subject. (*Takes lighter from pocket.*) Just an unimaginative nurse who decided she was in a position to kill folks off for their life insurance—and ran through quite a list before anybody suspected her. (*Lights cigarette.*)

EMORY. (*Lighting cigar.*) Was this recent?

18

TASKER. Well, last year and the year before. (*Crosses up to dining table for his glass.*) She'd be going still only she was too stupid to vary her poisons, with the result that all her victims had similar symptoms—(*Crosses down to* R. *end of sofa.*) nausea, burning throat, intestinal pain and convulsions—(*Christine fills his tea glass.*) to say nothing of the conventional life insurance policies made out to the old girl with the arsenic. (*He sits on stool.*)

CHRISTINE. (*Shuddering a little as she puts pitcher of tea on coffee table.*) Please, I don't like to hear about such things.

MONICA. (*Interested.*) You don't?

CHRISTINE. (*Picks up her glass.*) No.

MONICA. Now that's an interesting psychic block. (*Puts glass on coffee table.*) Why would Christine dislike hearing about murders?

CHRISTINE. I don't know—I have an aversion to violence of any kind. I even hate the revolver Kenneth keeps in the house.

MONICA. Oh, do you dislike the revolver more than the poisons?

CHRISTINE. I hate them both.

MONICA. Hmm, maybe if you'll try saying the first thing that comes into your mind, we can get at the root of the anxiety. Just say it, no matter how silly it seems to you! Tell your story, Reggie, and Christine will associate.

EMORY. Oh, nonsense, Monica.

CHRISTINE. What do you mean "associate"?

MONICA. Oh. (*Monica points to Tasker to go on with the story, as she listens closely.*)

TASKER. Well, the end of the story was like this. Toward the middle of May, last year, Mrs. Allison visited her sister-in-law's family. She got there in time for lunch, and her niece Shirley reminded her that she had promised to bring a present for her birthday. Mrs. Allison was so upset about forgetting the present that she went to the neighborhood store and bought candy and soft drinks for the family.

MONICA. (*Eagerly.*) Do you think of anything? (*Christine doesn't respond. Monica pokes her* L. *arm.*)

CHRISTINE. (*Turns to Monica.*) Oh, absolutely nothing. (*Monica points to Tasker to continue.*)

TASKER. Actually, Mrs. Allison *had* brought her niece a present. It was ten cents' worth of arsenic. (*Tasker and Emory laugh.*)

19

MONICA. (*To Christine.*) But there must be something in your mind—something!

CHRISTINE. (*To Monica.*) Well, I was thinking at the moment of how devoted the Fern sisters were to my father, when he was a radio commentator.

MONICA. (*She thinks this over.*) Hmm—I don't think I understand that—so far. (*To Christine.*) How did you know of this?

CHRISTINE. Oh, they told me when I entered Rhoda in their school.

EMORY. Isn't your father Richard Bravo?

CHRISTINE. Yes.

EMORY. I thought so. The whole nation was devoted to him during the last war.

TASKER. Yes, I listened to Bravo every evening.

MONICA. (*Anxious to get on with the story.*) Is there more of the story, Reggie?

TASKER. Uh-uh—when Mrs. Allison returned from the store she opened a bottle of sarsaparilla for her niece, and then watched the little girl's convulsions for an hour.

MONICA. (*Raises her hand to stop Tasker.*) Now—without thinking at all—what's your second association? (*Christine hesitates.*) No editing—no skipping ——

CHRISTINE. Well, what I was thinking then was even sillier. I've always had a feeling that I was an adopted child, and that the Bravos weren't my real parents.

MONICA. (*Lightly.*) Oh, you poor innocent darling! Don't you know that the changeling fantasy is the commonest of childhood? I once believed I was a foundling—with royal blood—Plantagenet, I think it was. (*Pointing to Emory.*) Emory was a Tudor. (*To Christine.*) But have you really always had this—suspicion—that you were adopted?

CHRISTINE. Yes, always.

MONICA. But no evidence?

CHRISTINE. Only that I dream about it.

MONICA. (*Eagerly.*) What kind of dream?

CHRISTINE. Oh, Monica, must I tell my dreams too? (*To Tasker.*) I'd rather hear the murder story. (*Christine, seeing Tasker needs ashtray, takes one off coffee table and puts it on R. arm of sofa.*)

20

MONICA. Well, let's hear more story, then hear more from Christine.

EMORY. Why do you always want to dig at people's insides? Monica, you're a ghoul.

MONICA. Of course, who isn't? Furnish the final details, Reggie.

TASKER. Well, Mrs. Allison hurried back to town on an urgent errand. She hadn't paid the current premium on the policy on Shirley's life, and this was the last day of grace.

EMORY. Stupid!

TASKER. Allison was certainly crude. But there have been artists in her line, really gifted operators like Bessie Denker. (*Christine, who has been looking at Tasker, suddenly turns front when she hears name.*) Bessie never made a mistake, never left a trace, never committed an imperfect crime ——

CHRISTINE. (*Suddenly interested.*) Who was this?

TASKER. The most amazing woman in all the annals of homicide, Bessie Denker. (*Christine slowly puts her glass on the table.*) She was beautiful, she was brainy and she was ruthless. She never used the same poison twice. Her own father, for example, died of rabies, contracted supposedly from a mad dog. It just happened that all his money went to Bessie ——

CHRISTINE. (*To Tasker.*) Did you say Bessie Denker?

TASKER. Yes. (*He takes a drink of his tea.*)

CHRISTINE. Excuse me. (*She rises, deep in thought, crosses R. to R. chair.*) I—I think—I ——

EMORY. (*Seeing that Christine is upset.*) I think Christine has had enough of this, Reggie. Couldn't we talk about something else?

TASKER. (*Watching Christine.*) We certainly could.

MONICA. And we will—though I'm still puzzled ——

CHRISTINE. (*Trying to right the situation.*) No, no—tell us more about Dr. Kettlebaum —— (*She sits in chair R.*)

EMORY. If you leave it to Monica, she has three subjects: sex, psychiatry and pills. Sex and psychiatry are synonymous. You better try pills.

MONICA. (*To Tasker.*) By pills Emory means the modern pharmaceutical discoveries which have revolutionized medicine since 1935. (*To Emory.*) If you took them, Emory, you'd be a better man.

TASKER. (*Looking at his watch—rises, crosses up to dining table.*) I should have looked at this before. (*Puts cigarette out in* ashtray on table, picks up coat from window seat.) I've got a lecture date at three-thirty, and I won't be much ahead of time if I start now. (Getting into coat, crosses R.) Will you forgive me for filling the air with horror stories, Mrs. Penmark?

CHRISTINE. (Rises, crosses up to meet Tasker.) Oh, you must forgive me, Mr. Tasker! (Emory rises from D. L. chair, crosses L. to open front door.) I have some kind of phobia or mania. I'm quite unreasonable when I hear such things.

TASKER. I'm sick of the bloody stuff myself and only keep on with it to make a living—so let's be friends. (He puts out a hand. Christine shakes with him.)

CHRISTINE. Yes, of course.

TASKER. I do have to go. (Crosses L. back of sofa. As he passes Monica.) Good-bye, Monica.

MONICA. Good-bye, Bluebeard.

EMORY. (Laughing as Tasker goes out front door.) Good-bye, Reggie. (Shouting after Reggie.) See you Sunday. I hear the red fish are running.

TASKER. (Offstage L.) Oh, good. (Christine is busy clearing some dishes from dining table. Emory closes door.)

EMORY. (Looking at watch.) I wonder if it wouldn't be about time for the news. (He goes to the radio above desk L.) Do you mind, Christine?

CHRISTINE. Of course not. I'll just clear these off. (She carries some dishes to the kitchen.)

MONICA. I'll lend a hand. (Monica rises, takes ashtray from arm of sofa and puts it on coffee table. She takes her glass and pitcher to kitchen. Emory finds the local news broadcast.)

THE RADIO. "Nothing more important has happened for many years in the field of foreign affairs." (Emory sits in desk chair. There is a brief pause, then the voice proceeds on a somewhat different note.) "I interrupt this broadcast to—I have been asked to announce that one of the children on the annual outing of the Fern Grammar School was accidentally drowned in the bay this afternoon." (Christine has heard this in kitchen and comes running out, followed by Monica.) "The name of the victim is being withheld until the parents are first notified. More news of the tragic affair is expected momentarily." (Christine turns in desperation to Monica, who clasps her shoulders. Emory turns the radio down.)

22

MONICA. It was not Rhoda. Rhoda is too self-reliant a child. It was some timid, confused youngster afraid of its own shadow. It certainly wasn't Rhoda.

THE RADIO. This is Station WNB in Tallahassee, bringing you the 3:15 news, brought to you by Pickets Hardware, best for your home needs.

(*Christine turns, standing above the stool. Emory stands, turns the radio up.*)

THE RADIO. "To return to local affairs, I am now authorized to give the name of the victim of the drowning at the Fern School picnic. It was Claude Daigle, the only child of Mr. and Mrs. Dwight Daigle of 126 Willow Street." (*Christine slumps to stool. Monica goes to her.*) "He appears to have fallen into the water from an abandoned wharf on the Fern property." (*Emory sits in desk chair.*) "It is a mystery (*They all rivet their attention to the radio.*) how the little boy got on the wharf, for all the children had been forbidden to play near or on it, but his body was found off the end of the landing, wedged among the pilings. The guards who brought up the body applied artificial respiration without result. There were bruises on the forehead and hands, but it is assumed these were caused by the body washing against the pilings. And now back to the national news." (*Emory rises and turns the radio off.*)

CHRISTINE. (*Rising.*) That poor child—poor little boy!

MONICA. (R. *of stool.*) They'll send the children home immediately. They must be on their way now.

EMORY. This will be the end of the picnic.

CHRISTINE. (*Between sofa and stool.*) I don't know what to say to her, Monica. Rhoda is eight. I remember I didn't know about death—or it didn't touch me closely—till I was much older. A teacher I adored died. My whole world changed and darkened.

MONICA. We'd better go. (*Crosses behind Christine to* U. L. *end of sofa.*) This is no time for well-meaning friends to look on from the sidelines.

CHRISTINE. (*Turning to Monica.*) Monica, I don't know what to say to her!

EMORY. (*Crosses* D., *takes his coat from back of* D. L. *chair.*) You'll meet it better alone. Honestly you will.

MONICA. (L. *end of sofa.*) Yes, you will, dear. We'll go. It's between you and Rhoda, now. Nobody else can help.

23

CHRISTINE. Yes, I suppose so.

EMORY. Children get these shocks all the time. (*Opens front door.*) Life's a grim business.

CHRISTINE. I'm glad you were here. (*Crosses* R. *below stool.*) She'll have missed lunch so I'll make her a sandwich.

MONICA. (*Crosses to door.*) We'll be upstairs in case you need us.

CHRISTINE. Thank you, Monica. Thank you both. (*Monica and Emory go out front door. Christine stands a moment thinking, then pulls herself together. Crosses to the coffee table, picks up an iced tea glass—goes to dining table and picks up a plate and another glass and exits to kitchen. Putting the dishes on the shelf she takes a loaf of bread from the bread box and disappears off* R. *After a moment Rhoda comes in the front door humming "Au Claire de la Lune"—she crosses behind the sofa to chair* R. *and sits. As she takes off her red shoes, Christine enters from the kitchen.*) Darling!

RHODA. Mother, you know we didn't really have our lunch because Claude Daigle was drowned.

CHRISTINE. (L. *of chair* R.) I know. It was on the radio.

RHODA. He was drowned, so then they were all rushing and calling and hurrying to see if they could make him alive again, but they couldn't, so then they said the picnic was over and we had to go home.

CHRISTINE. I'm glad you're home! (*Starts to reach toward Rhoda and is stopped by her question.*)

RHODA. So could I have a peanut-butter sandwich and milk? (*Christine kneels* L. *of chair and takes Rhoda by the arms.*)

CHRISTINE. Did you see him, dear?

RHODA. Yes, of course. Then they put a blanket over him.

CHRISTINE. Did you see him taken from the water?

RHODA. Yes, they laid him out on the lawn and worked and worked. But it didn't help.

CHRISTINE. I want you to get those pictures right out of your mind. I don't want you to be frightened or bothered at all. These things happen sometimes and when they do we simply accept them.

RHODA. I thought it was exciting. (*Christine takes her arms away.*) Could I have the peanut-butter sandwich?

CHRISTINE. (*Rising.*) Yes, I'm getting it ready for you. (*She goes into the kitchen. Rhoda puts shoes in cupboard under book-*

24

shelves U. L. and takes out skates and loafer shoes. Christine enters with a glass of milk and sandwich as Rhoda sits in chair D. R. Standing back of chair, she hands Rhoda the glass.) Here, dear. Darling, you're controlling yourself very well, but just the same it was an unfortunate thing to see and remember. I understand how you feel, my darling.

RHODA. I don't know what you're talking about. I don't feel any way at all. (She tastes the milk. Christine is puzzled. She crosses to L. of chair and puts the sandwich on the small table. Rhoda, seeing she has displeased her mother, rises and throws her arms around her waist, then takes her mother's hand and kisses it.)

CHRISTINE. (Takes Rhoda by the shoulders.) Have you been naughty?

RHODA. Why, no, Mother. (Stepping back.) What will you give me if I give you a basket of kisses?

CHRISTINE. (Feeling a great rush of affection, sits in chair R. and hugs Rhoda.) I'll give you a basket of hugs!

RHODA. (After a moment, feeling she has won her mother over.) I want to go out and skate on the asphalt.

CHRISTINE. (Rising.) Then you should, dear. (Christine rises and crosses toward the kitchen. She hesitates at the door and looks back at Rhoda who is putting on one of her skates. Christine is obviously puzzled at Rhoda's detached attitude about Claude's death. She shakes off her doubts and exits into kitchen closing the door behind her. Rhoda fastens the strap on her skate as Leroy enters the front door carrying a large cardboard box. He steps off the platform behind the sofa and looks at Rhoda.)

LEROY. (Under his breath.) How come you go skating and enjoying yourself when your poor little schoolmate is still damp from drowning in the bay? (Dumps trash in wastebasket behind sofa into box.) Looks to me like you'd be in the house crying your eyes out; (Crosses R. behind sofa toward Rhoda, stops behind chair R.) either that or be in church burning a candle in a blue cup. (Rhoda stares at Leroy, but gives no answer. Then with one skate in her hand, she gets up and skates on her one skate to the kitchen door.)

RHODA. (Sticking her head into the kitchen.) 'Bye, Mother!

CHRISTINE. (From the kitchen.) Good-bye, Rhoda. (Rhoda skates back to R. table and picks up sandwich.)

LEROY. (*Behind chair* R.) Ask me, and I'll say you don't even feel sorry for what happened to that little boy.

RHODA. Why should I feel sorry? It was Claude Daigle got drowned, not me. (*She skates toward the front door. Leroy shakes his head.*)

CURTAIN

ACT I

SCENE 3

It is evening of the same day.
Rhoda is ready for bed, lying on the sofa with a pillow under her head. There's a glass of apricot juice on the coffee table with two vitamins on a napkin beside it. Also a box of stationery, pen and half finished letter. Christine, in her robe, sits on the stool reading from Rhoda's book.

CHRISTINE. (*Reading.*) "Then the knight alit from his steed and sought what way he could find out of this labyrinth, and a path appearing he began to make his way along it and it began at that time to grow dark. The knight had not gone more than a dozen paces before he saw beside the path a beautiful lady who laid out a fair damask cloth under an oak and set thereon cates and dainties and a flagon with two silver cups." (*She looks up from her reading on the last few words deep in thought.*)

RHODA. (*Sitting up.*) Mommy?

CHRISTINE. (*Turning to her.*) Yes.

RHODA. Why aren't you reading?

CHRISTINE. (*Closing book.*) I was just thinking, I guess.

RHODA. What about? The accident?

CHRISTINE. (*Hesitates.*) Partly—and about my toll phone call. (*Indicating phone on desk.*) The circuits were busy. (*She opens book.*)

RHODA. What are cates and dainties?

CHRISTINE. (*She pauses—looks at book.*) Oh—little cakes, I think.

RHODA. Oh. (*Rhoda lies down again.*)

26

CHRISTINE. (*Reading.*). . . "and set thereon cates and dainties and a flagon with two silver cups. 'Knight,' she called, 'knight, come eat and drink with me, for you are hungry and thirsty and I am alone.' " (*To Rhoda.*) Did you take your vitamins, dear?

RHODA. (*Sitting up.*) I took one before. This is the second. I was saving them because I like the juice. (*Takes one pill and a sip of apricot juice. Then turns to her mother—sweetly.*) This is wonderful, to have you read to me out here.

CHRISTINE. You'd better take the third one now.—You'll be too sleepy.

RHODA. All right. (*She takes the other vitamin and the last of the drink, then lies back.*) I'll close my eyes, but I won't be asleep.

CHRISTINE. I know. (*She reads.*) "Then the knight answered her, 'I thank you, fair lady, for I am not only hungry and thirsty but I am lost within the forest.' Then he let his palfrey graze nearby and he feasted with the lady, who gave him loving looks, sweeter than the wine from the flagon, though the wine was sweet and strong, and in this fashion the time passed till the light was gone out of the wood and it was dark." (*She pauses and looks at Rhoda who has fallen asleep.*) "The knight heard the music of hautbois softly playing and he perceived that a fair pavilion stood nearby under the oak trees, lighted by a torch at the entrance where there were servants going to and fro. And he was aware that the pavilion had not been there in the daylight, but had been created out of darkness—by magic ——" (*Looks again at Rhoda and calls softly.*) Rhoda? Rhoda? (*There's no answer. Christine rises, puts book on coffee table, takes the empty glass to the kitchen, returns and bends over Rhoda, picks her up and carries her off R. She returns and as she passes C. stage looks off toward Rhoda's bedroom. She goes to the sofa and picks up a box of stationery off the coffee table and begins to write as the phone rings. She crosses to the desk quickly and answers the phone.*) Hello.—Yes, I did place a call to Washington, D. C. Mr. Richard Bravo—that's right—yes, Bethesda 7-1293. (*She sits desk chair.*) Daddy? I'm so glad I found you at home. I've been trying to get you all evening. Daddy—you said in your last letter that you might be coming to Tallahassee. Are you sure you're well enough to be doing such things?—Well, that's not really far from here. Couldn't you come to see me? Daddy, could you make it sooner? Could you —— Oh, no—we're both well. It's not that. Oh, you

27

met Kenneth at the airport? How is he? Tell him I love him and miss him very much. But, Daddy—I must see you —— No, it's nothing like that. Daddy, do you remember that recurrent dream I used to have when I was a little girl?—Now I'm beginning to have it again and again. I know what the Freudians say—but even they tell you dreams can't come out of any past but your own. Daddy, is there some terrible thing about my past that I don't know? No—nobody. It's something I dream. All right—I'll be good. And remember I love you. And tell Kenneth I'm finishing my first letter to him tonight, and I'll send it air-mail special in the morning. And, Daddy, I will see you, won't I? All right, dear. —Good night. (*She hangs up slowly—looks at the phone a moment deep in thought. She shakes it off—rises and returns to the sofa and sits. She picks up her letter and reads—then looks off* R. *toward Rhoda's bedroom—looks back at the letter and slowly tears it up as the curtain falls.*)

ACT I

Scene 4

A few days later, in the same apartment. The living-room is empty, Rhoda can be seen practising "Au Clair de la Lune" on the piano in the den. The book Christine was reading in the preceding scene has been removed, and another child's book has been put on D. R. *table. It is mid-morning. The doorbell chimes. On the second chime, Christine comes out of kitchen and crosses* R. *Seeing Rhoda in den she closes door, crosses and opens front door.*

MISS FERN. May I come in, Mrs. Penmark?
CHRISTINE. Yes, of course, Miss Fern. (*Miss Fern enters* L.) I meant to come and see you. I got your note. (*Christine closes front door.*)
MISS FERN. (*Crossing to sofa.*) We're in such distress, all of us at the school, and we've suffered such a blow, losing one of the children that way, I'm sure you'll excuse us for going over and over things!

CHRISTINE. (*Crosses to* D. L. *chair.*) I think everybody has been puzzled and worried and saddened.

MISS FERN. I don't think I've ever known any happening to puzzle so many people in so many ways. And I can help so few of them. (*Miss Fern sits on* R. *end of sofa.*) I've just come from seeing Mrs. Daigle. Of course, our first thought was of her. (*Christine sits on* U. S. *arm of* D. L. *chair.*) The rest of us are touched only lightly by this tragedy. She will have to live with it the rest of her days.

CHRISTINE. I know.

MISS FERN. I have seen her several times, and each time she has asked me to find out from you if you had any possible clue to where the penmanship medal might be. (*Piano stops.*)

CHRISTINE. Was it lost?

MISS FERN. Yes, it wasn't found with the body and has completely disappeared.

CHRISTINE. I didn't know of this. (*At this moment Rhoda comes out of the den, dressed immaculately as usual, crosses* C. *Christine, on seeing Rhoda, signals Miss Fern not to speak in front of her.*)

RHODA. (*Curtseying.*) Good morning, Miss Fern.

MISS FERN. Good morning, Rhoda.

RHODA. (*Picking up book from table next to* D. R. *chair. She crosses below coffee table. To Christine.*) Mother, could I sit under the scuppernong arbor for a while and read my book?

CHRISTINE. Of course, Rhoda.

RHODA. It's shady there, and I can see your window, and you can watch me from the window, and I like to be where you can see me.

CHRISTINE. (*Looking at book.*) Is it a new book?

RHODA. Yes. It's *Elsie Dinsmore*. The one I got for a prize at Sunday school.

CHRISTINE. I'll be here.

RHODA. I'll be right there all the time. (*Turns and curtseys to Miss Fern.*) Good-bye, Miss Fern. (*She exits out front door.*)

MISS FERN. (*She waits till Rhoda exits.*) It did occur to me that —that Rhoda might have told you a detail or two which she hadn't remembered when she talked with me. You see, she was the last to see the little Daigle boy alive ——

CHRISTINE. Are you sure of that?

MISS FERN. Yes.

CHRISTINE. I hadn't realized —— (*Christine rises, crosses and sits L. end of sofa.*)

MISS FERN. About an hour after we arrived at the estate one of our older pupils came on Rhoda and the Daigle boy at the far end of the grounds. The boy was upset and crying, and Rhoda was standing in front of him, blocking his path. The older girl was among the trees, and neither child saw her. She was just about to intervene when Rhoda shoved the boy and snatched at his medal, but he broke away and ran down the beach in the direction of the old wharf where he was later found. Rhoda followed him, not running, just walking along, taking her time, the older girl said.

CHRISTINE. Has it occurred to you that the older girl might not have been telling the truth?

MISS FERN. That isn't at all likely. She was one of the monitors we'd appointed to keep an eye on the younger children. She's fifteen and has been with us since kindergarten days. No, Mrs. Penmark, she was telling precisely what she saw. We know her well.

CHRISTINE. And this was the last time Claude was seen?

MISS FERN. Yes. A little later—it might have been about noon— one of the guards saw Rhoda coming off the wharf. He shouted a warning, but by then she was on the beach again and he decided to forget the matter. The guard didn't identify the girl by name, but she was wearing a red dress, he said, (*Christine looks toward front door.*) and Rhoda was the only girl who wore a dress that day. (*Christine rises slowly, looking toward door.*) At one o'clock the lunch bell rang and Claude was missing when the roll was called. You know the rest, I think.

CHRISTINE. (*Turns, crosses below coffee table to dining table looking out window.*) Yes. But this is very serious—if Rhoda was on the wharf ——

MISS FERN. Not serious, really, when you've seen as much of how children behave as I have. Children conceal things from adults. (*Christine crosses slowly D. C.*) Suppose Rhoda did follow the Daigle child onto the wharf—so many things could have happened quite innocently. He may have concealed himself in the old boat-house, and then, when discovered, may have backed away from Rhoda and fallen in the water.

CHRISTINE. Yes, that could have happened.

MISS FERN. Now, Claude, although he looked frail, was an excellent swimmer—and, of course, Rhoda knew that. Once he was in the water she would have expected him to swim ashore. How could she know that the treacherous pilings were at the exact spot where he fell?

CHRISTINE. No, she couldn't possibly . . .

MISS FERN. Perhaps the thought in Rhoda's mind when he fell in the water was that he'd ruin his new suit and she'd get a scolding for causing it. When he didn't swim ashore at once she may have thought, with the logic of childhood, that he'd hidden under the wharf to frighten her—or to escape her. Later on, when it was too late to do anything, she was afraid to admit what had happened.

CHRISTINE. Then you think Rhoda knows something she isn't admitting?

MISS FERN. Yes. I think that, like many a frightened soldier, she deserted under fire. (*Christine starts to reply.*) This is not a serious charge. Few of us are courageous when tested.

CHRISTINE. She has lied, though.

MISS FERN. Is there any adult who hasn't lied? Smooth the lines from your brow, my dear. You're so much prettier when smiling.

CHRISTINE. I shall question Rhoda.

MISS FERN. I wish you would, though I doubt that you'll learn more than you know.

CHRISTINE. (*Crosses, sits on stool.*) Miss Fern, there's something I want to ask you. There was a floral tribute at Claude's funeral sent by the children of the Fern School. I suppose the children shared in the expense—but I haven't been asked to pay any part of it.

MISS FERN. The tribute wasn't nearly so expensive as the papers seemed to think. The money has been collected, and the flowers paid for.

CHRISTINE. Perhaps you telephoned me, and I was out.

MISS FERN. No, my dear. We thought perhaps you'd want to send flowers individually.

CHRISTINE. But why should we have sent flowers individually? Rhoda wasn't friendly with the boy, and my husband and I had never met the Daigles.

MISS FERN. (*Flustered.*) I don't know, my dear. I really ——

31

There are three of us, you know, and in the hurry of making decisions —— (*She pauses.*)

CHRISTINE. You make excuses for Rhoda—and then you admit that you didn't ask me to help pay for the flowers—and the reasons you give for not asking are obviously specious. (*Rising and stands below stool.*) Does this mean that in your mind, and the minds of your sisters, there is some connection between the Daigle boy's death and Rhoda's presence on the wharf?

MISS FERN. I refuse to believe there is any connection.

CHRISTINE. And yet you have acted as if there were.

MISS FERN. Yes, perhaps we have.

CHRISTINE. This is a terrible tragedy for Mrs. Daigle, as you say. She has lost her only child. But if there were any shadow over Rhoda—from what has happened—I shall have to live under it—and my husband, too. As for Rhoda—she would not be happy in your school next year. (*Turns U. S. toward window.*)

MISS FERN. No, she would not. (*Christine stops and turns toward Miss Fern.*) And since she would not, it would be as well to make up our minds now that she will not be there.

CHRISTINE. (*Crosses D. C.*) Then there is a shadow over her— and you have already decided not to invite her back?

MISS FERN. Yes. (*Rises and faces Christine.*) We have made that decision.

CHRISTINE. But you can't tell me why?

MISS FERN. (*Crosses to Christine.*) I think her behavior in the matter of the medal would be sufficient explanation. She has no sense of fair play. She's a poor loser. She doesn't play the game.

CHRISTINE. But you're not saying that Rhoda had anything to do with the Daigle boy's death.

MISS FERN. Of course not! Such a possibility never entered our minds! (*At this moment the doorbell chimes.*)

CHRISTINE. I'd better answer.

MISS FERN. Of course, my dear. (*Christine goes to the front door, hesitates, looks back at Miss Fern who has crossed to chair R., and then opens front door. Mr. and Mrs. Daigle come in, he tentatively, she boldly. She has been drinking.*)

CHRISTINE. Yes.

MRS. DAIGLE. (*She barges in—stops and turns to Christine.*) Thanks. We're Mrs. Daigle and Mr. Daigle. You didn't have to let us in, you know. (*To Miss Fern as she crosses C.*) You realize

32

we followed you. We shouldn't have done it. I'm a little drunk. (*To Christine.*) I guess you never get a little drunk.

CHRISTINE. You're quite welcome, both of you. (*Christine closes door—after Mr. Daigle gives her apologetic look and he slowly crosses—L. of L. chair.*)

MRS. DAIGLE. (*At U. R. end of sofa.*) Oh, pay no attention to him. He's all for good breeding. He was trying to stop me. Now, you, Mrs. Penmark. You've always had plenty. You're a superior person.

CHRISTINE. No, I'm not. (*Crosses and stands in front of sofa.*)

MRS. DAIGLE. Oh, yes. Father was rich. Rich Richard Bravo. I know. Me, I worked in a beauty parlor. Miss Fern used to come there. (*Crosses R. to Miss Fern.*) She looks down on me.

MISS FERN. Please, Mrs. Daigle. (*Sits in chair R.*)

MRS. DAIGLE. I was that frumpy blonde. Now I've lost my boy and I'm a lush. Everybody knows it. (*Crosses C.*)

MR. DAIGLE. We're worried about Mrs. Daigle. She's under a doctor's care. She's not herself.

MRS. DAIGLE. (*To Mr. Daigle.*) But I know what I'm about just the same. Just the same. (*Crosses above stool to R. end of sofa.*) May I call you Christine? I'm quite aware that you come from a higher level of society. You prolly made a debut and all that. I always considered Christine such a gentle name. Hortense sounds flat—that's me, Hortense. "My girl Hortense," that's what they used to sing at me, "hasn't got much sense. Let's write her name on the privvy fence." Children can be nasty, don't you think?

MR. DAIGLE. Please, Hortense.

MRS. DAIGLE. You're so attractive, Christine. You have such exquisite taste in clothes, but of course you have amples of money to buy 'em with. (*Crosses D. L. to Christine in front of sofa.*) What I came to see you about, I asked Miss Fern how did Claude happen to lose the medal, and she wouldn't tell me a thing.

MISS FERN. I don't know, Mrs. Daigle. Truly.

MRS. DAIGLE. (*Turns and crosses quickly to Miss Fern.*) You know more than you're telling. You're a sly one—because of the school. You don't want the school to get a bad name. But you know more than you're telling, Miss Butter-Wouldn't-Melt Fern. (*Turns to cross L.—to stool.*) There's something funny about the whole thing. I've said so over and over to Mr. Daigle. He married quite late, you know. In his forties. 'Course I wasn't exactly what the fellow calls a "spring chicken" either. We won't have any more children. No more.

MR. DAIGLE. (*Coming around* D. L. *chair.*) Please, Hortense. Let me take you home where you can rest.

MRS. DAIGLE. Rest. (*Sits on stool.*) Sleep. When you can't sleep at night, you can't sleep in the daylight. I lie and look at the water where he went down. There's something funny about the whole thing, Christine. I heard that your little girl was the last one who saw him alive. Will you ask her about the last few minutes and tell me what she says? (*Christine looks at Miss Fern.*) Maybe she remembers some little thing. I don't care how small it is! No matter how small! (*Turns, looks at Miss Fern.*) You know something, Miss Fern dyes her hair. She knows something and she won't tell me. Oh, my poor little Claude! What did they do to you? (*Rises. Christine goes to Mrs. Daigle.*)

CHRISTINE. I will ask Rhoda, Hortense. Oh, if I only knew!

MRS. DAIGLE. (*Grabs Christine's arms.*) Somebody took the medal off his shirt, Christine. It couldn't come off by accident. (*Fingering Christine's dress.*) I pinned it on myself, and it had a clasp that locks in place. It was no accident. (*Looks at Christine's dress.*) You can wear such simple things, can't you? I never could wear simple things. I couldn't even buy 'em. When I got 'em home they didn't look simple.—He was such a lovely, dear little boy. He said I was his sweetheart. He said he was going to marry me when he grew up. I used to laugh and say, "You'll forget me long before then. You'll find a prettier girl, and you'll marry her." And you know what he said then? He said, "No, I won't, because there's not a prettier girl in the whole world than you are." If you don't believe me, ask the girl who comes in and cleans. She was present at the time. (*Christine puts her arms around Mrs. Daigle.*)

MR. DAIGLE. Hortense—Hortense!

MRS. DAIGLE. (*Stands back* U. C.) Why do you put your arms around me? You don't give a damn about me. You're a superior person and all that, and I'm—oh, God forgive me! (*Looks at her hands.*) There were those bruises on his hands, and that peculiar crescent-shaped mark on his forehead that the undertaker covered up. He must have bled before he died. That's what the doctor said. (*To Christine.*) And where's the medal? (*Crosses to Miss Fern.*) Who took the medal? (*Hitting chair.*) I have a right to know what became of the penmanship medal! If I knew, I'd have

34

a good idea what happened to him.—(*Turns to Christine.*) I don't know why you took it on yourself to put your arms around me. I'm as good as you are. And Claude was better than your girl. He won the medal, and she didn't.—I'm drunk. (*Crosses D. C.*) It's a pleasure to stay drunk when your little boy's been killed. (*Crosses to sofa.*) Maybe I'd better lay down. (*Lies down on sofa.*)

MR. DAIGLE. (*Helping Mrs. Daigle up.*) We'll go home, and you can lie down there. (*Christine helps raise Mrs. Daigle to a sitting position then crosses and opens front door.*)

MRS. DAIGLE. (*Rising, crosses to door.*) Why not? Why not go home, and lay down? Good-bye, all.

MR. DAIGLE. (*To Christine at door.*) I'm sorry.

MRS. DAIGLE. (*Giving him a little push.*) Oh, who cares what they think? (*Turns to Christine on platform.*) I drank a half bottle of bonded corn in little sips. I'm drunk as holy hell. (*The Daigles go out front door. Christine closes the door and crosses to D. L. chair.*)

CHRISTINE. Oh, the poor woman!

MISS FERN. (*Seated in chair R.*) I've tried to think of any little thing I could to tell her. But nothing helps.

CHRISTINE. Nothing will ever help.

MISS FERN. No.—(*Rises, crosses up C.*) I'll be getting back. (*Crosses behind sofa to L. end of sofa.*) Thank you for bearing with her, and with me.

CHRISTINE. I'll talk to Rhoda. I know there isn't anything that will help that poor creature—(*She indicates the front door.*) but I'll do what I can.

MISS FERN. We both have to do what we can. Good-bye, Mrs. Penmark. (*Offering her hand.*)

CHRISTINE. Good-bye, Miss Fern. (*Christine starts to take her hand—and suddenly embraces Miss Fern.*) She will have to live with it till she dies.

MISS FERN. Yes. Till she dies. Thank you. (*She goes out front door. Christine closes the door then turns and looks at the apartment, then goes to the window from which she can see Rhoda. After a moment she waves, and we know that Rhoda has looked up from her book. The telephone rings, and Christine answers.*)

CHRISTINE. Hello, yes, speaking.—Kenneth, oh, darling, (*She sits in desk chair.*) I'm so glad you called. The little boy who was drowned? Oh, no, Rhoda's her usual self. She's across the street where I can see her reading a book. I just waved to her. Do you really, darling?—I hope it won't be too much longer. Four weeks is a long, long time. Call me as often as you can. (*She looks toward the window.*) Kenneth . . . (*Pause.*) I love you. Then don't be late. Good-bye, dear. (*She bangs up. The door chimes and Monica enters front door, dressed to go out, carrying gloves and purse and smoking a cigarette.*) Oh, Monica.

MONICA. (*Closing door.*) Yes, Christine, the fluttery one with the typically inane conversation, but I do have an errand this time, not just gab ——

CHRISTINE. Come in, please. (*Stands above desk.*)

MONICA. (*Crosses to sofa.*) It's Rhoda's locket I'm using for an excuse. I've actually found a place where they'll change the stone and clean it in one day. (*Sits on sofa.*) They didn't agree to this unusual effort without a little pressure—in fact, I had to threaten ——

CHRISTINE. (*Crosses to window.*) Not really?

MONICA. (*Putting out cigarette in ashtray on coffee table.*) Oh, you don't know the old busybody. She uses pressure, influence, bribery, blackmail—(*Christine crosses D. C.*) and I had to pull them all on old Mr. Pageson. (*Turns to Christine.*) He said this little job would take at least two weeks ——

CHRISTINE. (*Crosses R. to Rhoda's table.*) I'll get the locket. I know where she keeps it.

MONICA. (*Putting on gloves.*) Good. I told him straight that I'm handling the Community chest again this year, and if he were as busy as all that, I'd be happy to revise my estimate of his contribution upward by a considerable amount. (*Christine has opened Rhoda's table drawer and found the locket in the chocolate box. She turns toward Monica, then looks back to drawer and lifts the edge of the drawer's felt lining, and sees the Penmanship Medal. She quickly closes the chocolate box and drawer and crosses to C. with the locket. Monica rises, crosses R. to Christine.*) Ah, you found it! The darling! She keeps her treasures so carefully it's a kind of miserly delight.

CHRISTINE. Shall I wrap it?

MONICA. No, no! I'll just drop it in my purse. (*She does so. Crosses below sofa to front door.*) And now I'll take to the air, dear Christine—only do forgive me for bursting in and rushing out!

CHRISTINE. No ceremony, please.

MONICA. Ceremony? No, just plain pragmatism! Good-bye, darling.

CHRISTINE. Good-bye, Monica. (*Monica goes out front door. Christine returns to the R. table, opens the drawer and takes out the medal. She looks at it with a kind of horror mixed with incredulity. After a moment she goes to the window from which Rhoda was seen. Evidently Rhoda is not there. She turns from the window and sits at couch, staring at the medal. The front door opens and Rhoda comes in quietly, and closes the door.*)

RHODA. (*Crosses, sits L. end of sofa.*) Did you want me to come in, Mother? When you waved?

CHRISTINE. (*She slaps the medal down on the coffee table.*) So you had the medal, after all. Claude Daigle's medal.

RHODA. (*Looking at the medal.*) Where did you find it?

CHRISTINE. How did the penmanship medal happen to be hidden under the lining of the drawer of your table, Rhoda? Now I want you to tell me the truth. (*Rhoda takes off one of her shoes and examines it. Then, smiling a little in a fashion she had always found charming, she asks—*)

RHODA. When we move into our new house can we have a scuppernong arbor, Mother? Can we, Mother? It's so shady, and pretty, and I love sitting in it!

CHRISTINE. Answer my question. And remember I'm not as innocent about what went on at the picnic as you think. Miss Fern has told me a great deal. So please don't bother to make up any story for my benefit. (*Rhoda is silent, her mind working.*) How did Claude Daigle's medal get in your drawer? It certainly didn't get there by itself. I'm waiting for your answer. (*Rhoda is silent.*)

RHODA. (*Innocently.*) I don't know how the medal got there, Mother. How could I?

CHRISTINE. (*Controlling herself.*) You know. You know very well how it got there. Did you go on the wharf at any time during the picnic? At any time?

RHODA. (*After a pause.*) Yes, Mother. I went there once.

CHRISTINE. Was it before or after you were bothering Claude?

RHODA. I wasn't bothering Claude, Mother. What makes you think that?

CHRISTINE. Why did you go on the wharf?

RHODA. (*Taking off her other shoe.*) It was real early. When we first got there.

CHRISTINE. Why did you go on the wharf? You knew it was forbidden.

RHODA. (*Picks up her shoes and looks at them.*) One of the big boys said there were little oysters that grew on the pilings. I wanted to see if they did. (*Rhoda hits the heels of her shoes together—Christine grabs them from her.*)

CHRISTINE. One of the guards said he saw you coming off the wharf. And he says it was just a little before lunch time.

RHODA. I don't know why he says that. He's wrong, and I told Miss Fern he was wrong. He hollered at me to come off the wharf and I did. I went back to the lawn and that's where I saw Claude. But I wasn't bothering him.

CHRISTINE. What did you say to Claude?

RHODA. (*Pause.*) I said—if I didn't win the medal, I was glad he did.

CHRISTINE. (*Rises, crosses C., turns back to Rhoda.*) Please, please, Rhoda. I know you're an adroit liar. But I must have the truth.

RHODA. (*Takes shoes, rises, crosses to Christine.*) But it's all true, Mother. Every word.

CHRISTINE. One of the monitors saw you try to snatch the medal off Claude's shirt. Is that all true? Every word?

RHODA. (*Crosses below Christine to her cupboard and puts her shoes on shelf and takes out her slippers.*) Oh, that big girl was Mary Beth Musgrove. She told everybody she saw me. Even Leroy knows she saw me. (*She opens her eyes wide, and smiles as though resolving on complete candor.*) You see, Claude and I were just playing a game we made up. (*Crosses to chair R., sits and puts on slippers.*) He said if I could catch him in ten minutes and touch the medal with my hand—it was like prisoner's base—he'd let me wear the medal for an hour. How can Mary Beth say I took the medal? I didn't.

CHRISTINE. (*Crosses to Rhoda.*) She didn't say you took the medal. She said you grabbed at it. And that Claude ran away down the beach. (*She sits on L. arm of chair R.*) Did you have the medal even then?

RHODA. No, Mommy. Not then. (*She turns to her mother and kisses her ardently. This time Christine is the passive one.*)

CHRISTINE. Rhoda, how did you get the medal?

RHODA. (*Crosses to stool.*) Oh, I got it later on.

CHRISTINE. How?

RHODA. (*Sits on stool.*) Claude went back on his promise and I followed him up the beach. Then he stopped and said I could wear the medal all day if I gave him fifty cents. (*She clicks her heels together.*)

CHRISTINE. Rhoda, stop that! (*Rises.*) Is that the truth?

RHODA. (*With slight contempt.*) Yes, Mother. I gave him fifty cents and he let me wear the medal.

CHRISTINE. Then why didn't you tell this to Miss Fern when she questioned you?

RHODA. (*Rises and runs to her mother.*) Oh, Mommy, Mommy! (*She whimpers a little.*) Miss Fern doesn't like me at all! I was afraid she'd think bad things about me if I told her I had the medal!

CHRISTINE. (*Kneels and holds Rhoda by the arms.*) Rhoda, you knew how much Mrs. Daigle wanted the medal, didn't you?

RHODA. Yes, Mother, I guess I did.

CHRISTINE. Then why didn't you give it to her?—(*Rhoda says nothing.*) Mrs. Daigle is heart-broken over Claude's death. It's destroyed her. I don't think she'll ever recover from it. Do you know what I mean?

RHODA. Yes, Mother, I guess so.

CHRISTINE. No. (*Christine takes her arms away from Rhoda.*) You don't know what I mean.

RHODA. But it was silly to want to bury the medal pinned on Claude's coat. Claude was dead. He wouldn't know whether he had the medal pinned on him or not. (*She senses her mother's sudden feeling of revulsion, and hugs her mother. Then gently strokes her neck.*) I've got the sweetest mother. I tell everybody I've got the sweetest mother in the world!—If she wants a little boy that bad, why doesn't she take one out of the Orphans' Home?

CHRISTINE. Rhoda! Get away from me! Don't talk to me. We have nothing to say to each other.

RHODA. Okay. Okay, Mother. (*She turns away and starts to den.*)

CHRISTINE. (*Rises.*) Rhoda! (*Rhoda stops and slowly turns front.*) When we lived in Baltimore, there was an old lady up-stairs, Mrs. Clara Post, who liked you very much.

RHODA. Yes. (*Crosses slowly down to back of sofa.*)

CHRISTINE. You used to go up to see her every afternoon. She was very old, and liked to show you all her treasures. The one you admired most was a crystal ball, in which opals floated. The old lady promised this treasure to you when she died. One afternoon when the daughter was out shopping at the super-market, and you were alone with the old lady, she somehow managed to fall down the spiral backstairs and break her neck. You said she heard a kitten mewing outside and went to see about it and somehow missed her footing and fell five flights to the courtyard below.

RHODA. (*At back of sofa.*) Yes, it's true.

CHRISTINE. (*Up* C.) Then you asked the daughter for the crystal ball. She gave it to you, and it's still hanging at the head of your bed.

RHODA. Yes, Mother.

CHRISTINE. (*Crosses, sits on stool.*) Rhoda, did you have anything to do, anything at all, no matter how little it was, with Claude getting drowned?

RHODA. (*Turns to Christine.*) What makes you ask that, Mother?

CHRISTINE. Come here, Rhoda. (*Rhoda crosses to Christine.*) Look me in the eyes and tell me. I must know.

RHODA. No, Mother. I didn't.

CHRISTINE. (*Pause.*) You're not going back to the Fern School next year. They don't want you any more.

RHODA. Okay. (*Turns away and plays with pillow on sofa.*)

CHRISTINE. (*Crosses to telephone. Sits in desk chair, dials the number.*) I'll call Miss Fern and ask her to come over.

RHODA. (*Running to her mother.*) She'll think I lied to her.

CHRISTINE. You did lie to her.

RHODA. But not to you, Mother! Not to you!

CHRISTINE. Hello, Fern School. (*Rhoda crosses slowly to stool.*) Miss Claudia Fern, please. No. No message. (*She hangs up and rises, crosses* U. S.) She's not home yet.

RHODA. (*Turns, looks at Christine.*) What would you tell her, Mother?

CHRISTINE. (*She looks at Rhoda a moment—then slowly shakes*

40

her head and crosses toward Rhoda.) No! It can't be true. (*She sits on stool facing* u. s. *and takes Rhoda in her arms.*) It can't be true. (*Rhoda puts her arms around Christine and looks over Christine's shoulder toward the audience with a very self-satisfied look as the curtain falls.*)

CURTAIN

ACT II

SCENE 1

SCENE: *The same apartment. Late afternoon, the next day.*

Rhoda is seated in chair R. at her little table putting a jigsaw puzzle together. She works with intense concentration, trying, rejecting, considering sizes and angles. As the curtain rises there is a knock on the front door and Monica enters carrying a cardboard box.

MONICA. Anybody here?

RHODA. Hello, Aunt Monica!

MONICA. Hi, honey. (*Closes door.*)

RHODA. (*Hollering off R.*) Mother!

MONICA. (*Crossing and meeting Christine C. stage as she enters from hall R.*) Oh, Christine! You said I might have Rhoda for a while. And there's a package for you.

CHRISTINE. (*Above stool.*) Thank you, Monica. You're always the bringer of gifts. (*She takes the carton from Monica and crosses D. C.*)

MONICA. (*Crosses between sofa and stool D. C.*) This is from somebody else. It was in the package room.

CHRISTINE. (*Looking at package.*) Oh—for Rhoda, from daddy ——

RHODA. (*Up at once and crosses to Christine.*) For me?

CHRISTINE. Oh, not yet. (*Reading from top of box.*) "In anticipation of her ninth birthday."

RHODA. What does anticipation mean?

MONICA. Looking forward to it.

CHRISTINE. "Not to be opened till ——"

RHODA. Oh. It's a long time to wait. But I will. (*She shrugs her shoulders and goes back to her chair.*)

MONICA. Isn't she the perfect old-fashioned girl? She'll wait!

42

CHRISTINE. No—there's more in daddy's writing—"Open when you get it—there'll be a real one later."

RHODA. (*Rises eagerly, crosses to them.*) But then he wants me to open it now!

CHRISTINE. Yes. All it needs is to be slit down this side with the scissors.

RHODA. (*Pulling excelsior out of end of box.*) There's excelsior —I can see it.

CHRISTINE. (*Picks up excelsior and hands it to Rhoda.*) Rhoda, it should be opened in the kitchen.

RHODA. Okay. (*She takes the package to the kitchen. Christine crosses to Rhoda's puzzle.*)

MONICA. (*Watching Rhoda, waiting till she's out of earshot.*) I wish she were mine! Every time I look at her I wish I had just such a little girl.

CHRISTINE. She's not wanted in the Fern School next year.

MONICA. Why?

CHRISTINE. She doesn't fit in, doesn't play the game. She's a poor sport. (*She sits in chair R. toying with jigsaw puzzle.*)

MONICA. Honestly, the longer I live, the more I see, the less I'm able to understand the tight little minds of people like the Fern girls. (*Crosses to table near R. chair for cigarette.*) The truth of the matter is, Rhoda is much too charming, too clever, too unusual for them! (*Picks up cigarette.*) She makes those others look stupid and stodgy by comparison! (*Offers one to Christine.*) Have one?

CHRISTINE. I seem to have quit.

MONICA. Seem to have! Good God, if I were to quit you'd hear the repercussions in New Orleans! (*Picks up matches.*) I string along with St. Paul —— (*Lights match.*) It's better to smoke than to burn. (*Monica lights cigarette. Christine laughs, rises, crosses to desk. Monica follows her a step or two.*) By the way could Rhoda stay up and have dinner with me tonight?

CHRISTINE. (*Standing above desk writing on pad.*) Yes, she could. I've asked Reginald Tasker over for cocktails and to talk to me about some writing I want to try.

MONICA. Fine, there's no reason why Rhoda should hear about his strychnines and belladonnas. (*Rhoda comes from the kitchen with a large pasteboard box in her hands and sits in chair R. Crosses to Rhoda.*) Rhoda, you're to have dinner with me tonight.

RHODA. I am? May I bring my new puzzle?

MONICA. You surely may.

CHRISTINE. Is that what it was? (*Monica sits L. of armchair R.*)

RHODA. I think it must be the best jig-saw puzzle in the whole world. (*There is a tap at the front door and as Leroy speaks it swings open.*)

LEROY. Leroy. (*Leroy enters with a garbage pail.*)

RHODA. Oh, Leroy, there was a lot of excelsior.

MONICA. He'll take care of it.

LEROY. Yes, surely, ma'am. (*Crosses and exits to kitchen.*)

CHRISTINE. (*At desk.*) Don't bother to sweep the kitchen. I'll do it.

RHODA. (*Holding puzzle up to show Monica.*) It's a map of Asia with all the animals. (*She puts puzzle on table R.*)

MONICA. I have an aversion to cobras, but it's Freudian. (*Leroy enters from kitchen carrying the empty cardboard box.*)

LEROY. There's a lot of this stuff scattered around, Mis' Penmark.

MONICA. Let him sweep it, dear. (*She rises and crosses L. to door. Leroy drops the box behind her in disgust. He goes back into kitchen.*) I shall run up and look at the simmering meat sauce.

RHODA. Oh, is it spaghetti?

MONICA. It is. Approve?

RHODA. My favorite!

MONICA. Come up any time. It must be nearly ready. (*She opens the front door, goes out and a Western Union Messenger is there.*)

MESSENGER. (*In the hall outside.*) Mrs. Penmark?

MONICA. Yes. This is her door. (*Monica looks in.*) Western Union for you, dear. (*Christine goes to door. Monica exits upstairs, leaving the Messenger in her place in the doorway. He hands Christine a yellow envelope and a pad which she signs.*)

CHRISTINE. Thank you.

MESSENGER. You're welcome.

CHRISTINE. (*She takes the envelope and the Messenger goes, closing the door. Christine opens the envelope, and reads the message with pleasure.*) Well!

RHODA. (*Working on her puzzle.*) Is it daddy?

CHRISTINE. Not your daddy this time; mine. He's coming here.

RHODA. Grandfather?

CHRISTINE. Yes. He'll be here tonight.—He can sleep—I think

44

Monica has an extra room—I'll run up and ask her! Be right back. (*She goes out front door. Leroy emerges from the kitchen again, sweeping a pile of excelsior. He pauses in the door—looks around to see if they're alone.*)

LEROY. (*Quietly as he sweeps.*) There she sits at her little table, doing her puzzle and looking cute and innocent. Looking like she wouldn't melt butter, she's that cool. She can fool some people with that innocent look she can put on and put off when she wants to, but not me. Not even part way, she can't fool me. (*He drops the broom—just missing her foot. She kicks at it, then turns back to the puzzle. As Leroy crosses to desk and returns with wastebasket.*) She don't want to talk to nobody smart. She likes to talk to people she can fool, like her mama and Mrs. Breedlove and Mr. Emory. (*Kneels on floor and puts excelsior in wastebasket.*)

RHODA. (*Seated in chair R., turns to Leroy.*) Go empty the excelsior. You talk silly all the time. I know what you do with the excelsior. You made a bed of excelsior in the garage behind that old couch, and you sleep there where nobody can see you. (*Goes back to her puzzle.*)

LEROY. I been way behind the times here-to-fore, but now I got your number, miss. I been hearing things about you that ain't nice. (*Begins sweeping.*) I been hearing you beat up that poor little Claude in the woods, and it took all three the Fern sisters to pull you off him. I heard you run him off the wharf. (*Jabs at her foot with broom.*) He was so scared. (*Jabs again.*)

RHODA. (*Kicks at the broom.*) If you tell lies like that you won't go to heaven when you die.

LEROY. I heard plenty. I listen to people talk. (*Picks up remainder of excelsior.*) Not like you who's gabbling all the time and won't let anybody get a word in edgewise. That's why I know what people are saying and you don't.

RHODA. People tell lies all the time. I think you tell them more than anybody else.

LEROY. I know what you done to that boy when you got him out on the wharf. You better listen to me if you want to keep out of bad trouble.

RHODA. What did I do, if you know so much?

LEROY. (*He pauses, looks at broom.*) You picked up a stick and hit him with it. (*Rises and strikes broom handle against palm.*) You hit him because he wouldn't give you that medal like you told

45

him to. I thought I'd seen some mean little girls in my time, but you're the meanest. You want to know how I know how mean you are? Because I'm mean. I'm smart and I'm mean. And you're smart and you're mean. (*Takes broom and puts it inside kitchen.*) And I never get caught and you never get caught.

RHODA. I know what you think. I know everything you think. Nobody believes anything you say.

LEROY. (*Returns from kitchen and closes door.*) You want to know what you did after you hit that boy? You jerked the medal off his shirt. Then you rolled that sweet little boy off the wharf, among them pilings.

RHODA. You don't know anything. None of what you said is true.

LEROY. (*Dumps excelsior from wastebasket to empty box he had dropped on floor earlier.*) You know I'm telling the God's truth. You know I got it figured out.

RHODA. (*Turns to him.*) You figured out something that never happened. And so it's all lies. Take your excelsior down to the garage and put it where you can sleep on it when you're supposed to be working.

LEROY. (*Looks up.*) You ain't no dope—that I must say—and that's why you didn't leave that stick where nobody could find it. Oh, no, you got better sense than that. You took that bloody stick and washed it off good, and then you threw it in the woods where nobody could see it.

RHODA. I think you're a very silly man.

LEROY. It was you was silly, because you thought you could wash off blood—and you can't. (*She pauses in her work, looks up.*)

RHODA. Why can't you wash off blood?

LEROY. Because you can't, and the police know it. You can wash and wash, but there's always some left. Everybody knows that. I'm going to call the police and tell them to start looking for that stick in the woods. They got what they call "stick bloodhounds" to help them look—and them stick bloodhounds can find any stick there is that's got blood on it. And when they bring in that stick you washed so clean the police'll sprinkle that special blood powder on it, and that little boy's blood will show up on the stick. It'll show up a pretty blue color like a robin's egg.

RHODA. You're scared about the police yourself!

LEROY. (*Rises, tries to quiet her.*) Shhh!

46

RHODA. What you say about me, it's all about you! They'll get you with that powder! (*Leroy hears Mrs. Penmark coming, crosses L. toward door.*)

LEROY. (*At L. end of sofa.*) As far as I'm concerned I wish there was more excelsior. I could use it.

CHRISTINE. (*She enters front door.*) What were you saying to Rhoda?

LEROY. Why, Mrs. Penmark, we was just talking. She said it was a big box of excelsior.

CHRISTINE. (*Seeing the anger on Rhoda's face, the smirk of triumph on Leroy's.*) Just the same you're not to speak to her again. If you do I'll report you! Is that entirely clear?

RHODA. (*Seated in chair R.*) I started it, mama. I told him it was a puzzle all about Asia, and I hardly know where anything is in Asia. (*Leroy crosses to front door, taking cardboard box of trash with him.*)

CHRISTINE. Very well—but don't speak to her!

LEROY. Yes, ma'am. (*He exits, closing door behind him.*)

CHRISTINE. (*Crossing toward kitchen.*) You're really working in the dark here. I think you strain your eyes working over these things, dear. (*Christine switches on lights L. of kitchen door and goes into kitchen and wheels a small bar out of the kitchen, set up to serve drinks, which she wheels over behind the sofa.*)

RHODA. (*As Christine crosses with her.*) Mother, is it true that when blood has been washed off anything a policeman can still find it was there if he puts powder on the place? Will the place really turn blue?

CHRISTINE. (*Turning to her.*) Who's been talking to you about such things? Leroy?

RHODA. No, mommy, it wasn't he. It was some men went by the gate in the park.

CHRISTINE. I don't know how they test for blood. But I could ask Reginald Tasker. Or Miss Fern, she might know.

RHODA. (*Jumps up.*) No—don't ask her! (*Realizes she's given herself away, she runs and grasps her mother around the waist.*) Mommy, mommy, mommy! (*She breaks down and cries, deliberately.*) Nobody helps me! Nobody believes me! I'm your little girl, and I'm all alone.

CHRISTINE. (*Holding her away.*) It's not a very good act, Rhoda.

47

You may improve it enough to convince someone who doesn't know you, but at present it's easy to see through.

RHODA. (*Wiping away tears with the back of her hand.*) Maybe I'd better go up to Monica's and have dinner.

CHRISTINE. Yes. She said any time. (*Rhoda turns and pushes her table back of its regular position D. R. Christine starts for the kitchen. As she reaches the door the doorbell chimes. She pulls the kitchen door shut and crosses L. She stops C. stage and looks back at Rhoda, who is looking in the mirror, arranging her braids. Christine crosses and opens the door revealing Reginald Tasker.*) Good evening, Mr. Tasker.

TASKER. (*Enters on platform.*) Good evening. (*Rhoda picks up new puzzle from table R. and crosses C.*)

CHRISTINE. This is my daughter, Rhoda.

TASKER. Hello, Rhoda. (*Crosses below sofa to Rhoda.*) Well, isn't she a little sweetheart!

RHODA. (*Making her curtsy.*) Thank you.

TASKER. That's the kind of thing makes an old bachelor wish he was married.

RHODA. You like little girls to curtsy?

TASKER. It's the best thing left out of the Middle Ages!

RHODA. I'm having dinner upstairs.

TASKER. (*Pulls her R. braid so that it hangs down in front of her shoulder.*) The loss is ours, all ours.

CHRISTINE. You may go now, Rhoda.

RHODA. Yes, mommy. (*She crosses toward door below coffee table carefully putting braid back over her shoulder and exits out front door.*)

TASKER. That's a little ray of sunshine, that one. Isn't she?

CHRISTINE. (*Closing door.*) I've seen her stormy.

TASKER. No doubt. But she's going to make some man very happy. Just that smile.

CHRISTINE. (*On platform.*) Since I called you I've had a wire from my father, and he'll be here tonight. It's a year since I've seen him. (*Crosses to bar.*)

TASKER. (*Crosses U. S. to bar behind sofa.*) Bravo's coming?

CHRISTINE. Yes.

TASKER. Now there's a man I always wanted to meet.

CHRISTINE. He may be here before long. He said perhaps for dinner.

TASKER. Good. By the way, if you're thinking of writing mystery stories Bravo was quite an authority on crime and criminals early in his career.

CHRISTINE. (*Puts ice in two highball glasses.*) Yes, I know he was.

TASKER. He could probably help you more than I could. Before he began covering wars he covered practically all the horror cases, from Leopold and Loeb on.

CHRISTINE. What will it be?

TASKER. Gin and tonic?

CHRISTINE. Good. I'll have it too. (*She takes gin from bottom shelf on bar—takes cap off and pours drinks. Tasker takes bottle opener and opens tonic.*) You see, what I wanted to ask was a psychological question and I doubt that it was asked or answered —if it has been—till recently.

TASKER. I may not know all answers.

CHRISTINE. Well, perhaps nobody does. (*Takes tonic from Tasker and mixes drink.*) But the story I was thinking of writing made me wonder—tell me, do children ever commit murders? Or is crime something that's learned gradually, and grows as the criminal grows up, so that only adults really do dreadful things? (*Hands tonic back to Tasker. He puts it on bar.*)

TASKER. Well, I have thought about that, and so have several authorities I've consulted lately. Yes, children have often committed murders, and quite clever ones too. Some murderers, particularly the distinguished ones who are going to make great names for themselves, start amazingly early.

CHRISTINE. In childhood?

TASKER. Oh, yes. Just like mathematicians and musicians. (*Crosses down, sits on* R. *arm of sofa.*) Poets develop later. (*Christine mixes her drink.*) There's never been anything worth while in poetry written before eighteen or twenty. But Mozart showed his genius at six, Pascal was a master mathematician at twelve, and some of the great criminals were top-flight operators before they got out of short pants and pinafores.

CHRISTINE. They grew up in the slums, or among criminals, and learned from their environment. (*The doorbell chimes.*) Oh—I wonder if that could be father! (*Sets drink on bar.*)

TASKER. (*Rising, crosses* R.) If it is I would like to stay and see him a moment ——

CHRISTINE. (*Crossing to front door.*) Oh, that's understood! (*She opens the door.*) Daddy! (*Bravo comes into the doorway, a man of fifty-five or sixty, handsome once, but somewhat stern and weary.*)

BRAVO. Hello, darling. I'm early. (*He sets small bag* D. C. *of door and hat on chair. Christine goes into his arms and they kiss, then stand looking at each other.*)

CHRISTINE. You're here! You're actually here!

BRAVO. (*Embrace again.*) I guess I'm something of a truant, sweetheart, but you said you wanted to see me, and I wanted to see you, so ——

CHRISTINE. I'm so glad! (*Suddenly realizes Tasker is present.*) This is Reginald Tasker, father.

BRAVO. (*Crosses below sofa, gives his hand to Tasker,* R. *of* C.) Ah, one of my favorites! (*Christine closes door and crosses to* R. *end of sofa.*)

TASKER. Puts you to sleep regularly?

BRAVO. Sometimes keeps me awake. You've done some impressive research for the Classic Crime Club.

TASKER. Now I've always thought the best papers they ever printed were by Richard Bravo.

BRAVO. That old dodo! No, no, he's written himself out, and talked himself out and now he's drifting round the country working for a second rate news service.

TASKER. You're really looking into this off-side oil?

BRAVO. That's what they've got me doing. But I took off and left them, for the moment anyway. I wanted to see my long-lost daughter. (*Christine crosses to him and puts her arm through his.*)

TASKER. I've sometimes wanted to ask you if you've ever considered coming back into the criminology racket. There's been nobody like you since you left.

BRAVO. Well, all compliments aside, my later books didn't sell as well as the early ones—and the war came along. Now I write filler.

TASKER. You've written some things that won't be forgotten.

BRAVO. Let's hope.

TASKER. And now your daughter is going to try her hand.

BRAVO. At writing? (*Looks at Christine.*) She can't even spell.

CHRISTINE. (*Crosses* L. *below sofa to up* R. *corner of sofa.*) I do

50

get lonely here with Kenneth away, and I thought I'd try to work out a murder mystery, in the evenings.

BRAVO. (*To Tasker.*) And you're encouraging this competition?

TASKER. Well, I was rather stumped by her last question. She was asking whether criminal children are always the product of environment.

BRAVO. Nothing difficult about that, little one. They are. Lock, can't I have some of this wicked mixture you're lapping up? (*Indicating bar, crossing to it.*)

CHRISTINE. (*Crosses up to bar, mixes drink.*) Of course, Daddy —I'm sorry. Do you really think they're always the product of environment?

BRAVO. (*At* R. *of her.*) Always.

TASKER. I couldn't prove you're wrong, of course. (*Crosses up* L. *of Bravo.*) But some doctor friends of mine assure me that we've all been putting too much emphasis on environment and too little on heredity lately. They say there's a type of criminal born with no capacity for remorse or guilt—born with the kind of brain that may have been normal among humans fifty thousand years ago——

BRAVO. Do you believe this?

TASKER. Yes, I guess I do.

BRAVO. Well, I don't. (*Takes drink from Christine, crosses down to* R. *end of sofa.*)

TASKER. I've been convinced that there are people—only a few, and certainly very unfortunate—who are incapable from the beginning of acquiring a conscience, or a moral character. Not even able to love, except physically. No feeling for right or wrong.

BRAVO. (*Crosses* D. S. *between sofa and stool.*) I've heard such assertions, but never found any evidence behind them. (*Sits* R. *end of sofa.*) If you encounter a human without compassion or pity or morals, he grew up where these things weren't encouraged. That's final and absolute. This stuff you're talking is tommyrot. (*He sips his drink.*)

CHRISTINE. Do your doctor friends have any evidence?

TASKER. They can't prove it yet, (*Crosses to* R. *end of bar.*) but they think there are such people. They say there are children born into the best families, with every advantage of education and discipline—that never acquire any moral scruples. It's as if they were born blind—you couldn't expect to teach them to see.

CHRISTINE. And do they look—like brutes?

51

BRAVO. (*To Christine.*) Are you sold on this?

CHRISTINE. I want to find out.

TASKER. Sometimes they do. But often they present a more convincing picture of virtue than normal folks. A wax rosebud or a plastic peach can look more perfect than the real thing. They imitate humanity beautifully.

CHRISTINE. But that's—horrible.

TASKER. Some of them seem to have done some pretty horrible things and kept on looking innocent and sweet.

BRAVO. I'd like to examine the evidence. Until we do there's not much sense discussing it.

TASKER. Well I'd like to go into it with you, Mr. Bravo. (*Crosses down, sits on stool.*) This clinic I frequent came long ago to the conclusion that there are bad seeds—just plain bad from the beginning, and nothing can change them.

CHRISTINE. (L. *of her.*) And this favorite murderess of yours— the one you were speaking of the other day—is she an instance?

TASKER. Bessie Denker —(*Bravo reacts to the name.*) was she a bad seed? Well, she may have been, because the deaths started so early in her vicinity. Bessie earned her sobriquet of "The Destroying Angel" in early childhood.

CHRISTINE. Oh, then she began young?

TASKER. Yes. The name wasn't applied to her till much later, when the whole story of her career came out, but Bessie was lethal and accurate from the beginning. One of her most famous murders involved the use of the deadly amenita, a mushroom known as "the destroying angel," and some clever reporter transferred the term to her.—In fact, it was a colleague of Mr. Bravo's, unless I've missed something ——

BRAVO. It may have been—I don't know.

CHRISTINE. How did she end?

TASKER. Well, Mr. Bravo knows more about it than I do ——

BRAVO. (*Rises, crosses* U. S. *center, tries to dismiss subject.*) I've forgotten the whole thing. Put it out of my mind. I'm in oil now. (*Sets glass on dining table.*)

CHRISTINE. (*To Tasker.*) Tell me—how did she end?

BRAVO. (*To Christine.*) You don't want to probe into this mess, sweetheart ——

CHRISTINE. Yes, I do.

BRAVO. Can't we change the subject?

CHRISTINE. No, darling, I want to know. What was the rest of the story, Mr. Tasker?

TASKER. There's the mystery. (*Rises, crosses up to her, pours more tonic in his drink.*) By the time the authorities got really roused about her she disappeared from the Middle West—just seemed to vanish. She had quite a fortune by that time. The fellow that seems to know most about her maintains that she went to Australia. A similar beauty emerged in Melbourne; (*Bravo lighting cigarette reacts to this news.*) her name was Beaulah Demerest, so if it was the same person she didn't have to change the initials on her linen or silver.

CHRISTINE. How could she—kill so many—and leave no trace?

TASKER. (*Turns to Bravo.*) You wrote a famous essay listing all her methods—you must know it better than I do ——

BRAVO. (*Crosses to chair R.*) Not at all. I've dropped all that—haven't read the recent literature.

CHRISTINE. Did she ever use violence?

TASKER. (*To Bravo.*) Forgive me, sir, I'll make it short. (*Bravo shrugs and sits in chair R. as Tasker crosses to bar.*) She made a specialty of poisons—studied not only drugs and toxins but the lives of those she wished to kill. It's practically impossible to prove murder when the victim dies of rattlesnake venom in Western Colorado. Too many diamond-backs about. And tetanus can be picked up in any barnyard. She made use of such things.—(*Crosses down, sits R. arm of sofa.*) It all came to a sudden end—she was indicted again and took off for parts unknown—leaving no—but wasn't there a child, a little girl? (*Christine crosses D. S. left of sofa.*)

BRAVO. Never heard of one. That must be a recent addition to the myth.

CHRISTINE. I wanted to ask one more question. (*Sits L. end of sofa.*) Was she ever found out here?

TASKER. Not in this country. Three juries looked at that lovely dewy face and heard that melting cultured voice and said, "She couldn't have done it."

CHRISTINE. She wasn't convicted?

TASKER. "Not guilty." Three times.

CHRISTINE. You think she was one of these poor deformed children, born without pity?

TASKER. Personally, I do.

CHRISTINE. (*Slowly.*) Did she have an enchanting smile?

TASKER. Dazzling, by all accounts.

CHRISTINE. She was—doomed?

TASKER. Absolutely. Doomed to commit murder after murder till somehow or other she was found out.

CHRISTINE. She'd been better off if she'd died young.

TASKER. (*Seated* R. *arm of sofa.*) And society would. And yet sometimes I wonder whether these malignant brutes may not be the mutation that survives on this planet in this age. (*Turns to Bravo.*) This age of technology and murder-for-empire. Maybe the softies will have to go, and the snake-hearted will inherit the earth.

BRAVO. (*In chair* R.) I'm betting on the democracies.

TASKER. And so am I. But we're living in an age of murder. In all history there have never been so many people murdered as in our century. Add up all the murders from the beginning of history to 1900, and then add the murders after 1900, and our century wins. All alone —— (*Puts drink on coffee table, rises—crosses* R. *to Bravo.*) And on that merry note I think I should take my leave, for I meant not to bother you and I've been lecturing.

BRAVO. (*Rises.*) You've got a highly questionable theory there— about heredity.

TASKER. I'd like to go into that with you when there's more time.

BRAVO. (*They shake hands.*) Let's do that next time I'm in town.

TASKER. Right. (*Crosses to Christine—shakes hands.*) And now I'll say good-evening, Mrs. Penmark—I'm afraid the pleasure's been all mine.

CHRISTINE. (*Precedes him to door.*) Not at all. I'll call you early in the week.

TASKER. (*At platform.*) I'm always about. (*To Bravo.*) Good-night, sir.

BRAVO. Good-night, Mr. Tasker.

CHRISTINE. Good-night. (*Tasker goes out, Christine closes door.*)

BRAVO. Are you really planning to write something?

CHRISTINE. I was just asking questions. (*Crosses and meets Bravo* D. C.) You saw Kenneth in Washington?

BRAVO. Yes. He's looking well. As well as possible when a fellow's hot, sticky, tired and most of all, lonesome.

CHRISTINE. We'd counted cn going somewhere this summer. Then there was a sudden change of orders.

BRAVO. (*Takes her by the shoulders.*) Am I looking too close, or is there something heavy on your mind?

CHRISTINE. Does something show in my face?

BRAVO. Everything shows in your face. It always did.

CHRISTINE. I'm not sure I'm worried about anything—now that you're here. (*Takes his hands in hers.*) I always felt so safe and comfortable when you were in the room. And you have the same effect now.

BRAVO. To tell you the truth you did a magic for me. I'd always wanted a little girl and you were everything lovely a little girl could be for her old dad. But, Christine. What did you want to ask me—that night you phoned?

CHRISTINE. (*Hesitates.*) Let me think a minute —— Would you like another drink? (*Crosses up to bar.*)

BRAVO. Yes, I guess I will. (*He gets his glass off dining-table.*) Let me fix something. Will you have more gin and tonic? (*He mixes drinks at the bar.*)

CHRISTINE. (*Crossing L. around sofa.*) No, thank you.

BRAVO. And speak up, darling. It's between us, whatever it is.

CHRISTINE. (*She sits L. end of sofa.*) My landlady here is—is a sort of amateur psychiatrist—a devotee of Freud, constantly analyzing.

BRAVO. I know the sort. (*Crosses D. S. R. of sofa.*)

CHRISTINE. Her name is Breedlove. You'll meet her, because she's offered a wonderful room for you to stay in while you're here. Rhoda's having dinner with her tonight.

BRAVO. You were going to come out with something.

CHRISTINE. Yes. Well, what I was going to ask reminded me of her. I confessed to her the other day that I had always worried about being an adopted child—had always been afraid that mommy wasn't really my mother and the daddy I love so much wasn't really my daddy.

BRAVO. What did she say?

CHRISTINE. She said it was one of the commonest fantasies of childhood. Everybody has it. She had it herself.

BRAVO. (*Sits R. end of sofa.*) It certainly is common.

CHRISTINE. But that doesn't help me. I still feel, just as strongly as ever, that old fear that you're not really mine.

BRAVO. Has something made you think of this lately?

CHRISTINE. Yes.

BRAVO. What is it?

CHRISTINE. My little girl, Rhoda.

BRAVO. What about her?

CHRISTINE. She terrifies me. I'm afraid for her. I'm afraid of what she may have inherited from me.

BRAVO. What could she have inherited?

CHRISTINE. Father—daddy—whose child am I?

BRAVO. Mine.

CHRISTINE. Daddy, dear, don't lie to me. It's gone beyond where that will help. I've told you about a dream I have—and I'm not sure it's all a dream. Whose child am I? (*He looks away.*) Are you my father? (*Bravo is silent. He rises, crosses slowly up center to dining table.*) This is a strange question to greet you with after being so long away from you—but I—I have to ask it. (*Rises, crosses to Bravo.*) And for Rhoda's sake—and mine—you must tell me.

BRAVO. What has Rhoda done?

CHRISTINE. I don't know. But I'm afraid.

BRAVO. It cannot be inherited. It cannot. (*He draws a deep breath, then takes a step and staggers slightly, putting out a hand for support.*)

CHRISTINE. Father, you're not well! (*She goes to him. He sinks to chair R. of dining table.*)

BRAVO. I'm all right, just get me a glass of water. (*She gets one from bar.*) Perfectly well. A trace of fibrillation once in a while, quite normal at my age. (*Christine hands drink to Bravo. He takes pill from pill-box and drinks.*) Thank you. And with fibrillation there's a slight dizziness, also normal. (*She takes glass, puts it on chest of drawers U. R.*) I'm all right now.

CHRISTINE. (*Up and L. of Bravo.*) I won't ask any more questions. I'm sorry.

BRAVO. I think that's better. Let's just close the book.

CHRISTINE. (*After a pause.*) Only I have the answer now.

BRAVO. The answer?

CHRISTINE. Yes.

BRAVO. (*With her hands on his R. shoulder.*) I've always been a very fortunate man, Christine. I could tell you a long history of jobs that came in the nick of time, of lost money found, of friends who showed up to pay old debts just when I had to have the money. At every main turning-point in my life some good fairy has seemed to intervene to flip things my way. And the biggest piece of luck I ever had—the luck that saved my reason and kept me going —was a little girl named Christine. (*Looks up at her.*) You were the only child I ever had. My life was futile and barren before you came, but you were magic for me, as I said, and you made life bearable. I changed my way of life—I wrote about other things, but I kept on—because of you.

CHRISTINE. You don't have to say any more.

BRAVO. I don't, do I?

CHRISTINE. You found me somewhere.

BRAVO. Yes. In a very strange place—in a strange way.

CHRISTINE. (*Crosses down to back of chair* R.) I know the place.

BRAVO. I don't think you could. You were less than two years old.

CHRISTINE. I either remember it or I dreamed it.

BRAVO. What kind of dream?

CHRISTINE. (*Above chair* R.) I dream of a bedroom in a farm house in a countryside where there were orchards. I share the room with my brother, who is older than I—and my—is it my mother?—comes to take care of him. She is a graceful, lovely woman, like an angel. I suppose my brother must have died, for afterward I'm alone in the room. One night I awake feeling terrified and for some reason I can't stay in that house. It is moonlight and I somehow get out the window, drop to the grass below and hide myself in the tall weeds beyond the first orchard. I don't recall much more except that toward morning I'm thirsty and keep eating the yellow pippins that fall from the tree—and when the first light comes up on the clouds I can hear my mother some distance away calling my name. I hide in the weeds and don't answer because I'm afraid. Is this a dream? Is it only a dream?

BRAVO. What name did she call?

CHRISTINE. It isn't Christine. It—it is—could it be Ingold?

BRAVO. You remember that name? (*Rises, crosses* D. S.)

CHRISTINE. Yes, it comes back to me. "Ingold! Ingold Denker," she . . . Denker!! Oh, daddy, you've concealed something from me all these years, haven't you? (*Crosses to Bravo* L. *of* R. *chair.*) I came out of that terrible household. You found me there.

BRAVO. The neighbors found you after your mother vanished. Where she went I never knew, nor did they, but she had quite a fortune by that time, and something had panicked her . . . so she

57

quickly got away. Leaving one child, an astonishingly sweet and beautiful little thing with the most enchanting smile I've ever seen. I was there covering the case for a Chicago paper and I wired my wife to join me. We couldn't resist you. (*She rushes to his arms.*)

CHRISTINE. Oh, daddy, daddy! Oh, God help me! (*Breaks away.*) Why didn't you leave me there? (*Crosses below R. chair up to kitchen door, leans against door jamb.*)

BRAVO. It was the neighbors found you and saved you. Would you rather have stayed with them?

CHRISTINE. (*Turning to Bravo.*) Oh, no, you know I wouldn't. You've been a wonderful father! But—that place—(*Crosses D. L. to sofa.*) and that evil woman—my mother ——!

BRAVO. (*Follows Christine.*) There are places and events in every man's life he'd rather not remember. Don't let it hurt you now. It's past and doesn't touch you.

CHRISTINE. (*Sits on sofa.*) I wish I had died then. I wish it. I wish it.

BRAVO. (*At R. end of sofa.*) It hasn't mattered where you came from! You've been sound and sweet and loving! You've given me more than I ever gave or could ever repay! If you'd been my own I couldn't have hoped for more! You knew nothing but love and kindness from us and you've given love and kindness, and sweetness all your life! Kenneth loves you, and you've made him happy. And Rhoda's a perfect, sweet, sound little girl!

CHRISTINE. (*Turns to Bravo.*) Is she, father? Is she?

BRAVO. What has she done?

CHRISTINE. (*Pause.*) She's—it's as if she were born blind!

BRAVO. It cannot happen. It does not happen. (*The doorbell chimes and Monica comes in front door. Bravo breaks R.*)

MONICA. (*Entering.*) Excuse me, please, but Rhoda has eaten her dinner, tired of her puzzle and now she wants a book..

CHRISTINE. We haven't even started yet.

MONICA. (*Crosses back of sofa. To Bravo C. S.*) And I haven't met Mr. Bravo. How do you do. (*Puts out her hand.*) I'm Mrs. Breedlove. The oversized analyst. I'm going to put you up, and promise not to annoy you.

BRAVO. You know what newspaper men are like—crusty, bitter, irascible. If you can put up with me you're a saint. (*Rhoda enters through front door.*)

RHODA. Granddaddy! (*Runs to Bravo.*)

BRAVO. Rhoda! (*Picks her up and puts her down.*)

MONICA. (U. C.) Isn't she perfection?

RHODA. Next to Daddy, you lift me up best! (*He stares at her face.*) Why do you look at me?

BRAVO. I want to see your face. (*Rhoda crosses to chair R. and sits. Bravo keeps looking at Rhoda.*)

MONICA. You know, Mr. Bravo, these Penmarks are the most enchanting neighbors I've ever had. Now I'll want Rhoda for dinner every night. (*He turns to Monica.*) Tell me, Mr. Bravo, didn't you write the *FINGERPRINT SERIES*?

BRAVO. I'm afraid I was very guilty of that about twenty years ago.

MONICA. I read the first volume to pieces, and wept over it till the parts I loved most were illegible—and then bought another!

BRAVO. I've finally met my public.

MONICA. I don't disappoint you? Anyway I'm large.

BRAVO. I like the way you read books to pieces. It's good for royalties.

CHRISTINE. (*Rises.*) It's time to get dinner for us.

BRAVO. Maybe I should find my room and get ready for the evening.

MONICA. (*Crosses back of sofa to front door.*) I'll take you up if you'd like to go now.

BRAVO. If you'll be so kind. (*He looks back at Rhoda—and then crosses to front door.*)

MONICA. (*In hall.*) It's the next floor above. Be back, Christine. (*Bravo picks up his bag and hat. Christine who has been trying to catch his reaction to Rhoda, looks at him as he stands in the doorway. He smiles at her and shakes his head, whispering "No." He goes out. Christine stands for a moment, slowly turns and looks at Rhoda who has been watching her. Rhoda rises, goes to her table, opens drawer and pretends to be busy. Christine exits to kitchen to prepare supper. Rhoda watches her disappear, then quietly closes the drawer and tiptoes to the kitchen door, looks in, then goes quietly out into hall R. She reappears with a brown paper bag, checks the kitchen again, then goes to the cupboard and picks up her shoes, dropping them into the bag. As she drops the second shoe into the bag Christine enters from kitchen. Rhoda closes the cupboard door and tries to hide the bag behind her. Christine stops and turns to Rhoda.*)

CHRISTINE. What are you doing?

RHODA. Nothing.

CHRISTINE. (*Indicating bag Rhoda holds.*) Is that for the incinerator?

RHODA. Yes.

CHRISTINE. What is it?

RHODA. (*Crosses L. in front of Christine.*) Some things you told me to throw away.

CHRISTINE. (*Grabs Rhoda's left arm.*) Let me see what's in the package.

RHODA. (*Rhoda tries to pull away.*) No.

CHRISTINE. Let me see it! (*She tries to take the bundle from a sullen Rhoda. Rhoda fights back. Christine holds on determinedly, and Rhoda begins to bite and kick like a little animal. The package tears, revealing Rhoda's shoes. Christine wrests the bundle away, and pushes Rhoda violently from her. Rhoda stares at her mother with cold, fixed hatred.*) You hit him with one of the shoes, didn't you? Tell me! Tell me the truth! You hit him with those shoes! That's how those half-moon marks got on his forehead and hands! Answer me! Answer me!

RHODA. (*After a silence, with contempt.*) I hit him with the shoes. I had to hit him with the shoes, Mother. What else could I do?

CHRISTINE. Do you know that you murdered him?

RHODA. It was his fault. If he'd given me the medal like I told him to I wouldn't have hit him! (*She sits in chair R. of dining table and begins to cry, pressing her forehead against table.*)

CHRISTINE. (*Crosses to L. of dining table and turns to Rhoda.*) Tell me what happened. Start from the beginning and tell me the truth. I know you killed him, so there's no sense in lying again. I want you to tell me the truth. (*She beats the last line out with the shoe on the table.*)

RHODA. (*Throwing herself into her mother's arms.*) I can't, Mother! I can't tell you!

CHRISTINE. (*Shaking Rhoda violently.*) Rhoda, I want —— (*She suddenly realizes what she is doing and stops, clasping her hands behind her.*) I'm waiting for your answer. Tell me. I must know now.

RHODA. (*Crosses to sofa.*) He wouldn't give me the medal like I told him to, that's all. (*Sits on sofa.*) So then he ran away from

60

me and hid on the wharf, but I found him there and told him I'd hit him with my shoe if he didn't give me the medal. He shook his head and said, "No," so I hit him the first time and then he took off the medal and gave it to me.

CHRISTINE. (*Standing above stool.*) What happened then?

RHODA. Well, he tried to run away, so I hit him with the shoe again. He kept crying and making a noise, and I was afraid somebody would hear him. So I kept on hitting him, Mother. I hit him harder this time, and he fell in the water.

CHRISTINE. (*Crosses, sits on stool.*) Oh, my God, my God! What are we going to do? What are we going to do?

RHODA. (*Rises, crosses to Christine and coquettishly strokes her mother's neck.*) Oh, I've got the prettiest mother! I've got the nicest mother! That's what I tell everybody! I say, "I've got the sweetest ——"

CHRISTINE. How did the bruises get on the back of his hands?

RHODA. He tried to pull himself back on the wharf after he fell in the water. But I wouldn't have hit him any more only he kept saying he was going to tell on me. (*Throws herself into her mother's lap. Christine hesitates, then clasps her daughter to her.*) Mommy, Mommy, please say you won't let them hurt me! (*Pause.*)

CHRISTINE. Nobody will hurt you. I don't know what must be done now, but I promise you nobody will hurt you.

RHODA. (*Pushing away from Christine—she rises and stands R. of Christine.*) I want to play the way we used to, Mommy. Will you play with me? If I give you a basket of kisses what will you give me?

CHRISTINE. (*Unable to bear it.*) Please, please.

RHODA. Can't you give me the answer, Mother? If I give you a basket of kisses ——

CHRISTINE. (*Pushing Rhoda away.*) Rhoda, go into your room and read. I must think what to do. (*Rhoda crosses R., takes book from table.*) Promise you won't tell anyone else what you've told me.

RHODA. (*With contempt.*) Why would I tell and get killed? (*Starts off R.*)

CHRISTINE. Rhoda —— (*Rhoda stops.*) What happened to old Mrs. Post in Baltimore? I know so much, another won't matter now.

RHODA. (*Crosses to chair* R.) There was ice on the steps—and I slipped and fell against her, and—and that was all.

CHRISTINE. That was all?

RHODA. (*Pause.*) No. I slipped on purpose.

CHRISTINE. Take the shoes and put them in the incinerator! Hurry! Hurry! Rhoda. Put them in the incinerator! Burn them quickly! (*Rhoda picks up the shoes and starts off* L. *Stops, returns to her mother.*)

RHODA. What will you do with the medal, Mother?

CHRISTINE. I must think of something to do.

RHODA. You won't give it to Miss Fern?

CHRISTINE. No, I won't give it to Miss Fern. (*Rhoda smiles—turns and walks slowly off* L. *as the* CURTAIN FALLS.)

ACT II

Scene 2

After breakfast in the apartment, the next morning. At rise the stage is empty and the phone ringing. The portable bar has been wheeled offstage to the kitchen. Leroy enters front door. He is carrying a garbage can.

LEROY. Leroy. (*He looks at phone, starts toward kitchen and decides to answer phone. Goes back and takes it off the hook and hangs up. As he goes into the kitchen the phone rings again.*) You'd better answer that phone. (*Rhoda emerges from kitchen carrying four ashtrays—puts one on dining table. She answers phone. Leroy stands in kitchen door with garbage can.*)

RHODA. Hello—no, Mr. Bravo isn't here. He's upstairs. Yes, I could write down a number. (*Writing on pad.*) Yes, sir.—I'll tell him. Goodbye. (*She leaves one ashtray on desk. Crosses* C. *to Leroy, who is moving* L. S. *At dining table.*) I found out about one lie that you told. There's no such thing as a "stick blood-hound."

LEROY. (*Crosses in front of her.*) I'm not supposed to talk to little Miss Goody-goody.

RHODA. Then don't.

LEROY. (*Stops, turns to her.*) Where's your Mama?

62

RHODA. (*Crosses—puts ashtray on table near chair* R.) Upstairs.

LEROY. (*Crosses to her.*) For your own sake, though, I'll tell you this much. There may not be any stick bloodhounds, but there's a stick. And you better find that stick before they do, because it'll turn blue and then they'll fry you in the electric chair.

RHODA. There wasn't any stick any more than there was any stick-bloodhounds.

LEROY. You know the noise the electric-chair makes? It goes z—z—z, and then you swivel all up the way bacon does when your mother's frying it.

RHODA. Go empty the garbage. (*She crosses* D. L., *clicking her heels as she goes. Puts ashtray on coffee table. Picks up book from sofa and sits down to read.*) They don't put little girls in the electric chair.

LEROY. (*Crosses* D. C.) They don't? They got a little blue chair for little boys and a little pink one for little girls. I just remembered something. Just the morning of the picnic I wiped off your shoes with the cleats on 'em. You used to go tap-tap-tap on the walk. How come you don't wear 'em any more?

RHODA. You're silly. I never had a pair of shoes like that.

LEROY. (*Crosses behind sofa.*) They used to go tap-tap when you walked and I didn't like it. I spilled water on 'em and I wiped 'em off.

RHODA. They hurt my feet and I gave them away.

LEROY. You know one thing? (*Puts garbage can on platform near desk—leans over back of sofa.*) You didn't hit that boy with no stick. You hit him with them shoes. Ain't I right this time?

RHODA. (*Ignoring him.*) You're silly.

LEROY. (*Crosses to* R. *end of sofa.*) You think I'm silly because I said about the stick. All I was trying was to make you say "No, it wasn't no stick. It was my shoes." Because I knew what it was.

RHODA. You lie all the time. All the time.

LEROY. How come I've got those shoes then?

RHODA. (*Looks up quickly.*) Where did you get them?

LEROY. I came in and got them right out of your apartment.

RHODA. (*Looking at book.*) It's just more lies. I burned those shoes. I put them down the incinerator and burned them. Nobody's got them.

LEROY. (*After a pause.*) I don't say that wasn't smart. That was. (*Sits on stool.*) Only suppose I heard something coming rattling

63

down the incinerator and I says to myself, "It sounds to me like a pair of shoes with cleats." (*Rhoda closes book slowly.*) Oh, I'm not saying you didn't burn 'em a little, but you didn't burn all of 'em up like you wanted to.

RHODA. (*Puts book down. Waits with a new frightening stillness and intensity.*) Yes? ——

LEROY. Now listen to this and figure out which of us is the silly one. I'm in the basement working, and I hear them shoes come rattling down the pipe. I open the door quick and there they is on top of the coals only smoking the least little bit. I grab them out. Oh, they're scorched some, but there's plenty left to turn blue and show where the blood was. There's plenty left to put you in the electric chair! (*He laughs a foolish little laugh of triumph.*)

RHODA. (*Calmly.*) Give me those shoes back.

LEROY. Oh, no. I got them shoes hid where nobody but me can find them.

RHODA. You'd better give me those shoes. They're mine. Give them back to me.

LEROY. (*Rises, in delight.*) I'm not giving them shoes back to nobody, see?

RHODA. (*Stands and stares at Leroy with cold fury.*) You'd better give them back to me, Leroy.

LEROY. (*Laughing.*) I'm keeping them shoes until —— (*His laughter dies under her fixed, cold stare. He begins to be afraid of her. He no longer wants to play this game.*) Who said I had any shoes except mine?

RHODA. You did. You get them and give them back.

LEROY. Now, listen, Rhoda, I was just fooling and teasing you. I haven't got any shoes. I've got work to do. (*He starts around sofa toward front door. Rhoda quickly moves up to door cutting off his exit.*)

RHODA. Give me back my shoes.

LEROY. I haven't got nobody's shoes. Don't you know when anybody's teasing you?

RHODA. Give them back!

LEROY. Go and practice your piano lesson! I haven't got 'em, I keep telling you. (*Rhoda turns, locks the door and whirls around. A cold fixed stare points at him.*)

RHODA. Will you bring them back!

LEROY. I was just fooling at first, but now I really believe you

64

killed that little boy. I really believe you did kill him with your shoes.

RHODA. You've got them hid, but you'd better get them and bring them back here! Right here to me! (*She shouts the last as footsteps are heard on the stairs off* L.)

LEROY. Quit talking loud, there's someone in the hall. (*He stops as if interrupted. Picks up the garbage can as Rhoda unlocks the door and runs to sofa, picks up book and sits reading.*)

CHRISTINE. (*Enters front door. She is wearing a sweater over her dress.*) What was Leroy saying to you?

RHODA. Nothing.

CHRISTINE. I heard you say, "Bring them back here."

RHODA. He said he had my shoes.

LEROY. (*At sofa below platform.*) I got nobody's shoes but my own. There's a number for Mr. Bravo to call. (*Indicates pad on desk.*)

CHRISTINE. You may go, Leroy.

LEROY. Yes, ma'am. (*He exits through front door. Christine moves* U. S. *to corner of desk, watching Rhoda. Bravo enters front door, Monica following closely behind. She carries Rhoda's locket.*)

CHRISTINE. Daddy, there is a message for you.

BRAVO. Thank you, sweetheart. (*Crosses up to desk, looks at pad.*) Oh yes! (*He takes the phone and dials.*)

MONICA. (*Crosses to Rhoda.*) Look what I have for you, Rhoda? Turquoise!

RHODA. (*Stands.*) Thank you, Aunt Monica.

MONICA. And here's the garnet too. (*Rhoda takes them, crosses* R. *to mirror and stands admiring the locket which she holds at her neck. Monica crosses to window seat and sits reading magazine she finds there. Christine crosses to* D. L. *chair, stands watching Rhoda.*)

BRAVO. Hello. Listen, Murry, I know I ran out on you but this was imperative. Just wouldn't wait.—When does it leave?—Yes, I've had breakfast. (*Christine turns and looks at Bravo.*) If I get a taxi now I could just make it.—Yes, I've never been on the rig. I'd like to see it. And remember I've never missed a deadline. Think nothing of it. (*He bangs up. To Christine.*) I'll be gone a couple of days,—(*Crossing to Monica, offering his hand.*)—but I plan to make this my headquarters the next few weeks if I may ——

MONICA. (*They shake hands.*) As long as you can stand us ——

BRAVO. (*Turns and calls Rhoda.*) Rhoda.

RHODA. (*Runs to him C. S.*) Yes, Granddaddy. (*He bends down and kisses her forehead. She gives him her most enchanting smile.*)

BRAVO. You ought to patent your smile. It does unfair things to your elders. (*Christine, unable to bear watching, turns and goes up to door. Rhoda turns away from Bravo and goes back to put the locket and stone in her drawer. Bravo crosses above sofa to Christine.*) I really have to go, dear. I'll pick up the taxi at the corner. (*He puts his arms on Christine's shoulders.*) You are the bright thing in my life, Christine. It was you I lived for. You I loved. No matter what happens I want you to remember that. (*He kisses her cheek.*) Don't worry. It will come out well.

CHRISTINE. Come back soon.

BRAVO. I will, sweetheart. My bag's upstairs. Don't come along. It'll be quicker. (*He goes out front door.*)

MONICA. What a trouper! (*Sound of ice-cream bells off L.*) Ah, the ice-cream man.

RHODA. Mother, could I have a popsicle?

CHRISTINE. (*Closes door—answers as though in a trance.*) Yes. Take the money from my purse. (*Rhoda runs into the kitchen. Christine crosses R., takes off her sweater and throws it in chair R. as she passes around it.*) It is hot today.

MONICA. (*Rises, looking out L. bay window.*) Yes, the streets seem deserted. (*Rhoda coming out of kitchen picks up matches from stove in kitchen. Christine observes this and stops her.*)

CHRISTINE. Rhoda, what have you got those for?

RHODA. (*Shaking match box.*) I guess I just wasn't thinking.

CHRISTINE. I'll take them, please. (*Rhoda hands the matches to Christine, who replaces them on stove in kitchen. Rhoda starts off toward door, as she gets to coffee table she stops—looks to see if her mother is looking and quickly grabs the matches off the coffee table and runs out the door. Christine comes wearily in from kitchen as Monica turns from the window.*)

MONICA. Christine, you won't mind too much if I'm nosey and ridiculous, but you haven't been yourself lately. It's as if something's dragging you down.

CHRISTINE. (*Sitting in R. dining chair.*) Does it show to other people?

MONICA. You mean you feel it?

CHRISTINE. Yes.

66

MONICA. Do you take vitamins regularly?

CHRISTINE. No.

MONICA. You should. That's one of the things we know. I have an awfully good combination, and I'll bring some down if I may. (*Sitting in* L. *dining chair.*)—And now you must really forgive me. Have you and Kenneth come to a parting of the ways? Is his secretary more to him than an expert on politics? Does she make a nest for him among the office buildings?

CHRISTINE. No, it's nothing like that, Monica. I wish I were as sure of other things as I am of Kenneth.

MONICA. Do you suspect some disease—something like cancer, for example? If you do we must face it and do everything that can be done. And a lot can be.

CHRISTINE. I'm perfectly healthy and sound as far as I know.

MONICA. Do you sleep enough?

CHRISTINE. Well, no. Not always.

MONICA. You must have some sleeping pills. That much we can do. And now I won't bully you any more, Christine. I'm only going to say that I love you truly and deeply, my dear, as though you were my own; in fact Emory feels that same way about you, but I needn't tell you that, for you know it already. (*Christine puts her head down on the table and cries.*) Tell me what it is, dear. You can trust me. (*Monica gets up, puts her arms around Christine, who weeps without restraint.*) Dear, dear Christine. You'll feel better now. Perhaps you can get some sleep. (*The doorbell chimes and Christine stirs herself slowly to answer it.*) Damn, I'll get rid of who ever it is. (*Monica goes to the front door and opens it. Mrs. Daigle stands in the door. Christine is near chair* R., *trying to control herself.*)

MRS. DAIGLE. Well, Mrs. Breedlove. Hi. (*Enters and crosses* R. *to front of sofa.*) You don't want me here, and I don't want to be here, but I can't stay away. So I got a little drunk and came over. (*To Monica.*) Excuse it, please.

MONICA. (*Closing door.*) You're very welcome. (*But the words come hard.*)

MRS. DAIGLE. Like a skunk. I know. (*To Christine.*) Mrs. Breedlove knows everybody. Knows even me. (*Monica crosses to* L. *chair and sits.*)

CHRISTINE. How are you, Mrs. Daigle?

MRS. DAIGLE. I'm half seas over, as the fellow —— (*Crossing to above stool.*) I just want to talk to your sweet little girl. She was one of the last to see my Claude alive.

CHRISTINE. Yes, I know.

MRS. DAIGLE. (*Looking about the room.*) Where do you keep the perfect little lady that was the last to see Claude? I thought I'd just hold her in my arms and we'd have a nice talk and maybe she'd remember something. Any little thing.

CHRISTINE. (*Steps u. s., indicating window.*) She's out playing.

MRS. DAIGLE. (*To Monica.*) I'm just unfortunate, that's all. Drunk and unfortunate. (*To Christine.*) Only she was right outside when I came by, ladies and gentlemen.

CHRISTINE. (*Going to the window.*) She isn't there now. I don't see her. (*But she couldn't for her life, call Rhoda.*)

MRS. DAIGLE. She's a perfect little lady, never gives any trouble, that's what I heard. Have you got anything to drink in the house? Anything at all. (*Christine goes to the kitchen.*) I'm not the fussy type. (*Mrs. Daigle crosses toward kitchen.*) I prefer bourbon and water but anything will do. (*Christine wheels bar out of kitchen and puts it behind sofa.*) Oh, ain't we swank? Really Plaza and Astor! (*Crosses, takes the top off the bottle, picks up a glass and crosses down to sofa.*) What I came here for was to have a little talk with Rhoda, because she knows something. I've called Miss Fern on the telephone a dozen times, but she just gives me the brushoff. She knows something, all right. (*She sits rather clumsily on sofa.*)

CHRISTINE. (*Crosses around to R. end of sofa.*) Oh, are you all right there?

MRS. DAIGLE. (*To Christine.*) I'm not intoxicated in the slightest degree. Kindly don't talk down to me, Mrs. Penmark. I've been through enough, without that. (*Starts pouring her drink as the front door opens and Rhoda enters, with her popsicle. As Mrs. Daigle sees her she puts the glass and bottle on the coffee table and watches Rhoda. Monica rises.*)

RHODA. I brought back change, Mother. (*Puts change in ashtray on coffee table.*)

CHRISTINE. Very well. Mrs. Daigle wants to see you.

MRS. DAIGLE. (*Looking at Rhoda.*) So this is your little girl? Claude spoke of you so often, and in such high terms. You were one of his dearest friends, I'm sure. He said you were so bright in school. So you're Rhoda.

RHODA. Yes.

MRS. DAIGLE. Come let me look at you, Rhoda. Now how about giving your Aunt Hortense a big kiss? (*Rhoda gives her popsicle to Monica and goes dutifully to be kissed. Mrs. Daigle takes Rhoda in her arms and pulls her down on the sofa and kisses her.*) You were with Claude when he had his accident, weren't you, dear? You're the little girl who was so sure she was going to win the penmanship medal, and worked so hard. (*Christine, unable to bear watching this, crosses up to dining table, facing the window.*) But you didn't win it after all, did you, darling? Claude won the medal, didn't he? Now tell me this: would you say he won it fair and square or he cheated? These things are so important to me now he's dead. Would you say it was fair Claude had the medal? Because if it was fair why did you go after him for it?

RHODA. (*Reaching toward Monica.*) I want my popsicle. (*Monica takes Rhoda's arms, trying to get her away from Mrs. Daigle, who holds tight.*)

MONICA. Rhoda, if you're going shopping with me, you'll have to come now. Mr. Pageson is going to show us his collection. (*Mrs. Daigle rises with Rhoda, hanging on to Rhoda's waist.*)

MRS. DAIGLE. Right now? (*Monica disengages Rhoda from Mrs. Daigle and ushers her out of the room through front door.*)

MONICA. We're a little late as it is. Bring your popsicle, Rhoda. You can wash upstairs.

MRS. DAIGLE. (*Standing by sofa.*) Well, I must say!

CHRISTINE. (*Turns and crosses* D. C.) They do have an appointment.

MRS. DAIGLE. I'm sure they do, or practically sure. (*Sits on sofa, pours drink.*) Of course. I didn't know Rhoda had all these social obligations. I thought she was like any little girl that stayed home and minded her mother, and didn't go traipsing all over town with important appointments. I'm sorry I interfered with Rhoda's social life. I'm sorry, Christine, and I offer my deepest apologies. I'll apologize to Rhoda too when I can have an interview with her. (*Drinks.*)

CHRISTINE. You haven't interfered at all. (*The telephone rings. Christine crosses above sofa and answers it.*)

MRS. DAIGLE. (*While Christine goes to the phone.*) I wasn't going to contaminate Rhoda in the slightest degree, I assure you.

CHRISTINE. Hello—hello—oh yes, Mr. Daigle. Yes, she's here. Not at all. (*Hangs up.*)

MRS. DAIGLE. Did you tell him I was drinking and making a spectacle of myself? Did you tell him to call the patrol wagon?

CHRISTINE. (*Crosses down to L. end of sofa.*) You heard what I said. I said only that you were here. Your husband said he was in the drugstore on the corner.

MRS. DAIGLE. I was just going to hold her in my arms and ask her a few simple questions.

CHRISTINE. Perhaps another time would be better.

MRS. DAIGLE. You think because I'm lit, but I'm not lit in the slightest degree, I assure you. But Rhoda knows more than she's told anybody, if you'll pardon me for being presumptuous. I talked to that guard, remember. It was a long interesting conversation, and he said he saw Rhoda on the wharf just before Claude was found among the pilings. She knows something she hasn't told, all right. (*Christine turns away to D. L. chair.*) I know what you're thinking. You're thinking, "How can I get rid of this pest?" You may fool some with that mealy mouth, but you look like "Ned in the primer" to me.

CHRISTINE. Then perhaps you'd better not come here again.

MRS. DAIGLE. (*Rises, picks up bottle and glass, starts R., around sofa.*) I wouldn't come here again for a million dollars laid out in a line! I wouldn't have come this time if I'd known about Rhoda's social obligations. (*Puts glass and bottle on bar. Christine turns to her.*) I won't wait for Mr. Daigle. I'll go home by myself. I know where I'm not wanted, and I'm not wanted in a place where people have all these social obligations, if you get what I mean. You're looking sort of sick and sloppy. (*Crosses D. to Christine.*) Come over to my house and I'll give you a free beauty treatment if you're pressed for ready cash. It won't cost you a nickel. (*The doorbell rings and Christine helps Mrs. Daigle sit on arm of sofa and then opens the front door. Mr. Daigle is there.*)

MR. DAIGLE. (*Enters, stands D. S. of front door.*) Thank you, Mrs. Penmark. Come, Hortense, it's time to go home.

MRS. DAIGLE. (*Rises, starts out.*) Oh, my God, oh, my God, it's time to go home! (*Turning, she weeps noisily, and embraces Christine at the door, resting her head on Christine's shoulder.*) Oh, Christine, Christine, you know something! You know something, and you won't tell me! (*The Daigles go out front door. Christine*

70

closes the door, stands for a moment, thinking, then goes to the phone and dials the operator.)

CHRISTINE. *(Into the phone.)* Operator, I want to call Washington, D. C. *(She covers the speaker.)* Kenneth, darling, Kenneth, my dear love, what can I say to you? That our daughter is a —— *(With great effort she speaks into the phone.)* Never mind, operator, cancel the call. *(She hangs up. There is a knock on the front door. It opens and Monica comes in carrying two small bottles of pills. She shuts the door, looks quickly around. Christine sits in desk chair, wiping her eyes with her handkerchief.)*

MONICA. Good, she's gone. Sweet, I know I shouldn't take things into my all too capable hands, but I couldn't let her paw Rhoda any longer.

CHRISTINE. Mr. Daigle came for her.

MONICA. And I fear I've loosened discipline just a little. I let Rhoda go down for another popsicle.

CHRISTINE. Did she want a second? That's most unusual.

MONICA. She seemed quite eager. And since she's not one of these fat and self-indulgent little blobs I doubt that it can do any harm.—By the way, here are the sleeping pills and the vitamins, both plainly marked. *(Christine takes the bottles, crosses above sofa and puts them in spice cabinet R. of kitchen door.)*

CHRISTINE. Thank you, Monica. I'll keep them separate.

MONICA. *(Crosses R. above sofa toward Christine.)* Emory called while I was upstairs. He's coming by with Reggie Tasker to store some fishing equipment they bought this morning, so I'll get lunch for them. Wouldn't you like to run up and eat with us—you and Rhoda both?

CHRISTINE. *(At spice cabinet, turns to Monica.)* Monica—I'd—I'd rather not, really.

MONICA. You poor girl, I do bully you, and I promised not to! *(Offstage R.: two muffled shouts—"Fire"—"Fire.")*

CHRISTINE. What was that?

MONICA. It sounded a little like somebody shouting, "Fire!" It sounded close by. *(Monica crosses up to L. window, looks out. Christine crosses C. Two other voices are now heard shouting, this time much nearer, and they are definitely crying "fire.")*

EMORY. *(Off R.)* Fire! Fire!

TASKER. *(Off R.)* Fire! Emory! This way! *(Rhoda comes in front door. She has finished her second popsicle, and goes calmly to the den.)*

CHRISTINE. (*Crosses* C.) Rhoda, who was shouting?

RHODA. I don't know, Mother.

CHRISTINE. It sounds as if there were a fire!

RHODA. I don't think so, Mother. (*She goes to den, closes door, and begins to play the scales. Christine crosses* R. *of dining table to* C. *bay window, looks out.*)

TASKER. (*Off* R.) Fire! Fire!

EMORY. (*Off* R.) Fire! Fire! The garage door! (*There is general confusion and other voices add to the calling.*)

TASKER. (*Off* R.) There's a man in there!

MONICA. They're going to break down the garage door.

VOICES. Break the door down! Is anybody in there! Fire! Fire! That's Leroy's door! Break it down! Fire! I can hear him! Break it down! Break it down! One! Two—Three —— (*There is a sudden ragged crash off* R., *as if a door were split from top to bottom, and a man's screaming, as if he were in extreme pain.*)

LEROY. (*Screaming unintelligibly off* R.) I haven't got 'em! I wasn't gonna do nothing! I was just saying it to tease you! I haven't got 'em, I never had 'em, I was just —— Oh, God, oh God!

MONICA. (*Turns to Christine.*) There's a man on fire!

CHRISTINE. (*Starts around dining table.*) His clothes are burning! His hair is burning! (*The piano continues to tinkle.*)

MONICA. (*Grabs Christine across table and pulls her back to window.*) Emory's there—and Reggie! (*Leroy screams—silence. Piano and voices stop.*)

CHRISTINE. (*Slumps to* R. *end of window seat. Monica shuts curtains, turns* D. S.) It's too late! He fell just before he got to the pond! (*Voices, low, off* R.—"Somebody get an ambulance"— "Looks like he's dead," *etc.*) He's lying still!

MONICA. (*At* L. *of dining table.*) Whatever can be done will be done. (*Offstage voices out.*)

CHRISTINE. I should have known it was coming! I should have known! (*Piano starts slowly playing "Au Claire De La Lune."*) Why am I so blind?

MONICA. Thank God Rhoda was in the den playing the piano, and heard none of this!

CHRISTINE. The fire was in the garage! Where Leroy was!

72

MONICA. There's nothing we can do.

CHRISTINE. This time I saw it! I saw it with my own eyes. (*Monica tries to calm her. In a mild hysteria.*) Tell them to stop screaming! It won't help to scream!

MONICA. Christine, Christine! You aren't making sense!

CHRISTINE. Tell her to stop the piano—and stop the screaming—I can hear it still, the man is still screaming, Monica, still screaming, and the piano going on and on while he's dying in fire, screaming, screaming a man's scream! (*The doorbell chimes and someone knocks at front door.*) I don't want to see anybody now.

MONICA. Wait, wait, dear —— (*Crossing to front door.*) It's probably Emory and Reggie, dear. (*Christine remains sobbing on the window seat, Monica opens the door.*)

EMORY. (*Sticking head in door.*) Everything all right?

MONICA. (*Crosses to upper L. end of sofa.*) Come in. (*Emory and Reggie come in, coats off and somewhat disarranged from a sudden encounter with fire-fighting.*)

EMORY. (*Near desk.*) We thought you'd be here. It was just a flare-up in the garage; it's out now, but I guess Leroy ——

MONICA. (*Turns and tries to stop him.*) Never mind ——

CHRISTINE. (*Seated on window seat.*) You can say it. I know about Leroy—I saw him burning. I saw him run down the walk and die! Could there be any worse than that?

TASKER. (*Near door.*) I guess you did see the worst of it, Mrs. Penmark. What seems to have happened is that he fell asleep on a bed he'd made out of excelsior, down in the garage, and his cigarette set fire to the stuff.

EMORY. And excelsior burns like gasoline when it's dry. (*Siren.*)

MONICA. (*Motioning them out.*) You'd better leave me alone with Christine for a minute.

TASKER. (*Exits through front door.*) That will be the ambulance.

EMORY. We can take care of that. (*Exits and closes front door behind him.*)

MONICA. (*Crosses to L. end of dining table.*) Now, Christine . . . (*The tune continues in the den, slightly faster.*)

CHRISTINE. (*Beating table.*) Monica, Monica! I can't bear it! I can't bear it! She's driving me mad! (*She leaps up and runs toward the den.*) How can she play that tinkle now? (*Trying door, which is locked.*) Rhoda! Rhoda!

73

MONICA. (*At* L. *dining chair.*) What is it, Christine? What is it?
CHRISTINE. (*Turns to Monica.*) It's heartless; I can't bear it!
I can't, I tell you. (*She goes to den door and beats on it with her fists.*) Rhoda! Rhoda! Will you stop that music! (*But it continues. Monica crosses and pulls Christine away, and forcing her down toward bar.*)
MONICA. Try to make sense, dear! (*The music stops abruptly.*)
CHRISTINE. (*Above bar.*) Rhoda! Rhoda! Stop that music! (*Rhoda comes out of the den, wide-eyed and innocent.*)
RHODA. Is Mommy sick, Monica? (*Christine tries to get to Rhoda but Monica holds her. As they struggle above bar.*)

CHRISTINE. Don't let me get	MONICA. Christine, she's only
my hands on her. You didn't see	a child. Christine, please, be
it. You could look away and	sensible. Christine—Christine—
play the piano, but it happened.	

MONICA. (*Pushing Christine away* R.—*so she stops* R. C.) What has she done!
CHRISTINE. (*Pauses.*) It's not what she's done—(*Crosses* D. R. *to* R. *chair.*)—it's what I've done.
RHODA. (*On platform.*) What does she mean, Monica?
MONICA. (*To Rhoda.*) I don't know, Rhoda. (*To Christine.*) She'd better have lunch upstairs with me, Christine. (*Crossing back of sofa to Rhoda.*) She'll stay till you're calmer.
CHRISTINE. Yes, take her, take her. (*She sinks into* R. *chair, shivering. Monica motions Rhoda toward front door and she goes and opens it.*)
MONICA. (*To Christine.*) Will you be all right?
CHRISTINE. Yes, I'm all right. Only the screaming goes on and on. (*She covers her ears.*)
MONICA. (*At door.*) We'll come down for you. Come, Rhoda. (*They go out front door. Christine still sits, shivering, and her voice drops to a moan.*)
CHRISTINE. She killed him —— But she's my little girl and I love her —— Oh, my baby, my baby! (*She puts her head in her arms and weeps silently.*)

CURTAIN

ACT II

Scene 3

After dinner in the apartment, the same day.
Rhoda, ready for bed, lies on the sofa. Christine, some-
how, has recovered her poise. She is also in her robe ready
for bed, and sits on stool reading.

CHRISTINE. (*Reading.*) "Polly put one toe out from under the covers to find out how cold it was, and it was nipping cold. She remembered why she had wanted to wake up, and got out of bed very softly, shivering and pulling on her dress and her stockings. She had never seen a Christmas Tree decorated and lighted the way they are at Christmas in houses where children have fathers and it isn't hard times. She had promised herself that she would see one." (*Christine pauses, looks at Rhoda and takes bottle of pills from pocket of robe.*) You have some new vitamins to take tonight.

RHODA. (*Sitting up and turns to Christine.*) New ones?

CHRISTINE. Yes. (*Takes cap off bottle.*)

RHODA. Are those the vitamins?

CHRISTINE. Yes.

RHODA. (*Stretches out hand.*) May I see them, please?

CHRISTINE. Yes, of course. (*Christine gives Rhoda the bottle, and she examines it closely.*) They're some that Monica sent down for us.

RHODA. Okay, Mommy. (*Rhoda gives bottle back to Christine.*) I think Monica likes me.

CHRISTINE. I'm sure she does.

RHODA. Swallowing pills is just a trick.

CHRISTINE. You're very good at it. (*Pause—Christine starts dumping pills into Rhoda's hand.*)

RHODA. Do you love me, Mommy?

CHRISTINE. Yes.

RHODA. Mommy, do you know about Leroy?

CHRISTINE. Yes.

RHODA. You told me to put my shoes in the incinerator, didn't you?

CHRISTINE. Yes.

RHODA. Did you do something with the medal?

CHRISTINE. (*She has about 12 pills in her hand—replaces cap on bottle and puts it in pocket of robe.*) I drove out to Benedict today to see Miss Fern. And then I made an excuse to go on the pier alone—and dropped the medal in the deep water there.

RHODA. (*She sighs in relief.*) Mommy, Leroy had my shoes, and he said he was going to give them to the police and then tell them about me—and they'd put me in the electric chair. So—I had to ——

CHRISTINE. (*Turns to Rhoda.*) You don't need to say any more.

RHODA. Will you read more now?

CHRISTINE. Yes, but first you have to take these. (*Christine rises, puts book on stool and sits on R. arm of sofa—holds her hand with pills toward Rhoda.*)

RHODA. So many?

CHRISTINE. (*Reassuring.*) They're a new kind. I'm to take them, too. (*Christine looks away. Rhoda takes four pills and picks up glass of apricot juice from up R. corner of coffee table. She takes a sip.*)

RHODA. I like apricot juice. It doesn't even need ice. (*Takes four more pills and a sip of juice. Pauses.*) Mommy, I took another box of matches, and I lit the excelsior and I locked the door. It wasn't my fault, Mommy. It was Leroy's fault. He shouldn't have said he'd tell the police about me and give them my shoes.

CHRISTINE. (*Unable to bear it, turns to her.*) I know.

RHODA. (*She takes the rest of the pills and drinks once more.*) There. That's all. (*Rhoda leans back against the back of sofa and closes her eyes. Christine looks at her empty R. hand—closes it and slowly brings it up to her heart. Rhoda quickly throws her arms around her mother's neck.*) Don't let them hurt me, Mommy.

CHRISTINE. (*Hesitates, then grasps Rhoda to her.*) I won't let them hurt you. (*She kisses Rhoda on the cheek.*) Goodnight.

RHODA. Goodnight, Mommy. Now will you read to me?

CHRISTINE. Yes. (*Christine rises slowly, picks up book and sits on stool. Rhoda fixes pillow and lies down on sofa. Christine watches, gathers her strength and begins reading.*) "When Polly was all dressed she found her shawl and crept very quietly out of the room and out the front door. The door creaked, and she waited and listened, but nobody woke up. She closed the door carefully and looked at the bright moon and the shining, cold snow. The Carters must have a tree. They lived two blocks away, and if they left the curtains open you could look in and see it. If only there weren't any dogs. Polly walked carefully on the hard snow on the walk, keeping the warm shawl close around her. It was further than she remembered to the Carters' house, but she could see that there were lights in the windows. She came near it, only making a little creaking noise on the snow, and stood for a while in front of the house before she dared go near. (*Christine pauses and looks at Rhoda, who is now asleep—she gathers her courage and continues reading.*) Then she gathered all her courage and walked across the yard, her shoes sinking through the crust. The Christmas Tree was right in the front window, and the lights were on in the house, so she could see the fruits and bells and strings of popcorn and candy—and the silver star at the top." (*Christine pauses again and looks at Rhoda. She makes no sign, and her breathing is deep and regular. Christine rises, lays down the book on stool, crosses to coffee table, picks up empty glass, crosses to kitchen, puts it on stove. Crosses to L. of dining table.*) Rhoda, dear, Rhoda, dear—you are mine, and I carried you, and I can't let them hurt you. I can't let them take you away and shut you up. They'd put you in some kind of institution. Nobody can save you from that unless I save you. So sleep well, and dream well, my only child, and the one I love. I shall sleep too. (*She gathers Rhoda up in her arms gently, and carries her into the bedroom. After a moment she returns and opens a drawer in a spice cabinet high on the wall R. of kitchen door, takes out a ring of keys and goes to the den. The stage is empty for 10 seconds, then a shot is heard off in the den.*)

Beat
Blackout

CURTAIN

ACT II

Scene 4

A few days later.
As the curtain rises Monica is seen coming from the kitchen with a coffee tray. The sun is shining through the windows but the stage is not brightly lit. As Monica nears the coffee table the front door opens and Emory, Kenneth and Tasker enter. Kenneth crosses toward the dining table.

MONICA. I've made coffee if anybody wants it. (*Crosses back to kitchen.*)
EMORY. (*Crosses, sits c. of sofa.*) That's a thought.
TASKER. I'm in favor. (*Closes front door, crosses to u. s. arm of d. l. chair. Kenneth puts his cap on r. dining chair and stands at dining table looking out the window.*)
MONICA. (*Coming from the kitchen with a plate of small sandwiches.*) Kenneth, coffee?
KENNETH. No, thanks, Monica. (*Sits on dining table. Monica puts sandwiches on table behind d. r. chair and stands back of chair. Pause.*) Now I must face living without her. Somehow I could almost believe she was still with me till they lowered that coffin into the earth—and I knew I'd never see her face again. Now the earth is empty, and I'm empty.
EMORY. She's left all of us feeling pretty much the same way.
KENNETH. (*Rises, crosses d. s. to r. of stool.*) And why did she do it? Why, in God's name, did she do such a thing? She wasn't unhappy when I left! (*Turns, crosses to Monica.*) Monica, she was closer to you than anyone else lately, did she say anything—that was any kind of a reason?
MONICA. I've gone over and over everything she said, till I'm almost distracted—and it just doesn't fit any pattern! And I've talked to everybody who knew her—and they're just incredulous and shocked. There seems to be no reason at all!
KENNETH. There was a reason. Christine didn't do things with-

78

out a reason. (*Turns, crosses center. To Tasker.*) Her father died suddenly, you said?

TASKER. (*Seated on* U. S. *arm of* D. L. *chair.*) He'd had a series of attacks and the news of Christine's death seemed to have been too much for his heart.

EMORY. (*On sofa.*) She had some worry or other and I think it was connected with her father.

TASKER. I think she brooded over the Daigle boy's death and about the death of Leroy.

MONICA. She was hysterical at the time of the fire. But that was understandable.

KENNETH. (*Turns, crosses to Monica.*) When it happened how did you find her? Did you hear the shot?

MONICA. Yes—we heard it—and ran down. She'd shot herself after giving Rhoda a deadly dose of sleeping pills. She had obviously planned that they should die together.

KENNETH. (*Turns, crosses* L. *to stool. To Tasker.*) Could she—could Christine have been insane?

TASKER. No. We can rule that out. I talked with her not long ago. She shuddered somewhat—at my murder cases—but her comments were completely level-headed.

EMORY. No, Christine wasn't crazy.

KENNETH. (*Sits on stool.*) I don't know how I'll live. I don't know that I will.

EMORY. I guess nothing helps.

KENNETH. Nothing.—I don't think it's much good without Christine. The army—and promotion—and—a career—it was Christine that kept me afloat—not any of that.

EMORY. She was a wonderful girl.

KENNETH. And she left me—crept away into the earth—and I don't know why! (*His voice breaks, and he chokes down an uncontrollable sob.*) I'm sorry. (*Rises, crosses up to dining table.*)

MONICA. You cry if you feel like it. She was worth it.

KENNETH. (*Leaning on table facing* U. S.) She didn't want to live. (*Beat. The piano begins playing off in den slowly, ghostlike "Au Claire De La Lune." Kenneth slowly looks toward den. At the end of first four bars Monica turns, crosses to Kenneth, puts her hand on his arm.*)

MONICA. Kenneth, you have a lot to be grateful for. If we hadn't heard the shot you'd have lost Rhoda too. (*Monica goes to*

79

den. Kenneth crosses D. R. *near chair and turns toward den. Monica opens the den door and calls.*) Rhoda. (*The piano stops— Rhoda enters and stands on edge of platform. The stage gets brighter.*)

RHODA. Did you like it, Daddy? I played it for you.

KENNETH. Oh, Rhoda. (*He kneels and holds out his arms. Rhoda runs to them.*) My Rhoda—(*Holding her at arm's length.*)— there's a little of Christine left! It's in your smile!

RHODA. I love you, Daddy! (*She steps back.*) What will you give me for a basket of kisses?

KENNETH. For a basket of kisses? (*He looks at her.*) Oh, my darling—I'll give you a basket of hugs! (*She runs to his arms and he holds her with her face over his shoulder smiling out toward the audience.*)

CURTAIN

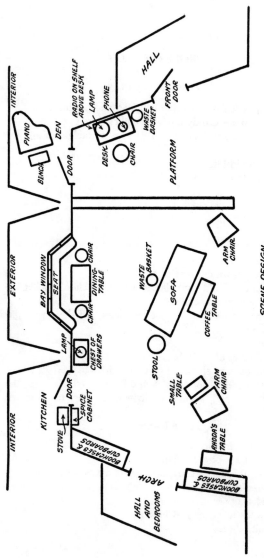

SCENE DESIGN
"BAD SEED"

81

PROPERTY PLOT

Throughout Play

On desk: Lamp, telephone, writing pad, pen and pencils
In Rhoda's table D. R.: Candy box with child's things in it
Cigarettes, ashtrays and matches on desk, D. R. table, dining table and coffee table
Matches on stove in kitchen
Mirror over Rhoda's cupboard D. R.
Pillows on sofa
Radio on shelf above desk U. L.
Wastebasket D. R. of desk

Act I—Scene 1

Trash in wastebasket
Small toy dog L. on windowseat U. C.
Off L. for Monica: Child's sunglasses with case, child's locket
Kenneth's Army hat on L. chair
Rhoda wears red and white dotted Swiss dress, red shoes with pieces of metal on heels
Book for Rhoda
Kenneth: 2 suitcases off R. In breast pocket: Ticket
Christine: Kenneth's briefcase off U. L. in den
2 small baskets, covered, for Monica and Rhoda—off L.
Leroy: Newspaper, pail, sponge, equipment for washing windows

Act I—Scene 2

Tasker's coat on windowseat
Emory's coat on back of D. L. chair
Cigar in pocket of Emory's shirt; matches in his coat pocket
Luncheon dishes, ashtrays, etc., on dining table
Glasses of iced tea
Pitcher of iced tea in kitchen—Christine
On table: Fruit, cheese
Matches in Tasker's coat pocket
Emory—wrist watch
Tasker—wrist watch

82

In kitchen: Shelf for dishes
Bread box with bread
In kitchen: Glass of milk, sandwich on plate
Off L. for Leroy: Large cardboard box for collecting trash
In Rhoda's cupboard D. R.: Roller skates, Rhoda's loafer shoes

ACT I—SCENE 3

Glass of apricot juice on coffee table; by it 2 vitamin pills on napkin
Box of stationery, pen and letter on coffee table
Christine: Child's book

ACT I—SCENE 4

Rhoda's slippers in her cupboard D. R.
On D. R. table: Copy of "Elsie Dinsmore"
Monica: Cigarette, gloves and purse
Gold medal and locket in chocolate box in drawer in Rhoda's table
D. R.

ACT II—SCENE 1

Off in kitchen for Rhoda: Cardboard box with jigsaw puzzle
Jigsaw puzzle on Rhoda's table D. R.
Monica: Cardboard box filled with excelsior
Leroy: Garbage pail
Western Union Messenger: Telegram, pad and pencil
In kitchen: Broom, small portable bar with glasses, liquor, bottle
    opener, ice, bottle of tonic, water in pitcher
Bravo: Small bag, hat, pill in pill-box
Offstage R.: Brown paper bag for Rhoda
In Rhoda's cupboard D. R.: The red shoes she wore in Scene 1—Act I

ACT II—SCENE 2

The ashtrays have been removed from desk, table D. R., dining table
    and coffee table
Offstage U. R. for Rhoda: 4 ashtrays
Leroy: Garbage can
On windowseat: Magazine
Monica: Rhoda's locket
Christine: Sweater over her dress
Check to be sure matches are on stove in kitchen and on coffee table
Offstage in kitchen: Money for Rhoda
Portable bar in kitchen, loaded as described above
Popsicle off L. for Rhoda

Coins off L. for Rhoda
Monica—2 small bottles of pills off L.

Act II—Scene 3

Christine: Book
Bottle of pills in pocket of Christine's robe
Glass of apricot juice on coffee table
Ring of keys in drawer in spice cabinet R. of kitchen door

Act II—Scene 4

Tray of coffee, cups, sugar in kitchen
Tray of sandwiches in kitchen
Kenneth: Army hat

NEW PLAYS

★ **THE CREDEAUX CANVAS by Keith Bunin.** A forged painting leads to tragedy among friends. "There is that moment between adolescence and middle age when being disaffected looks attractive. Witness the enduring appeal of Prince Hamlet, Jake Barnes and James Dean, on the stage, page and screen. Or, more immediately, take a look at the lithe young things in THE CREDEAUX CANVAS…" –*NY Times*. "THE CREDEAUX CANVAS is the third recent play about painters…it turned out to be the best of the lot, better even than most plays about non-painters." –*NY Magazine*. [2M, 2W] ISBN: 0-8222-1838-0

★ **THE DIARY OF ANNE FRANK by Frances Goodrich and Albert Hackett, newly adapted by Wendy Kesselman.** A transcendently powerful new adaptation in which Anne Frank emerges from history a living, lyrical, intensely gifted young girl. "Undeniably moving. It shatters the heart. The evening never lets us forget the inhuman darkness waiting to claim its incandescently human heroine." –*NY Times*. "A sensitive, stirring and thoroughly engaging new adaptation." –*NY Newsday*. "A powerful new version that moves the audience to gasps, then tears." –*A.P.* "One of the year's ten best." – *Time Magazine*. [5M, 5W, 3 extras] ISBN: 0-8222-1718-X

★ **THE BOOK OF LIZ by David Sedaris and Amy Sedaris.** Sister Elizabeth Donderstock makes the cheese balls that support her religious community, but feeling unappreciated among the Squeamish, she decides to try her luck in the outside world. "…[a] delightfully off-key, off-color hymn to clichés we all live by, whether we know it or not." –*NY Times*. "Good-natured, goofy and frequently hilarious…" –*NY Newsday*. "…[THE BOOK OF LIZ] may well be the world's first Amish picaresque…hilarious…" –*Village Voice*. [2M, 2W (doubling, flexible casting to 8M, 7W)] ISBN: 0-8222-1827-5

★ **JAR THE FLOOR by Cheryl L. West.** A quartet of black women spanning four generations makes up this hilarious and heartwarming dramatic comedy. "…a moving and hilarious account of a black family sparring in a Chicago suburb…" –*NY Magazine*. "…heart-to-heart confrontations and surprising revelations…first-rate…" –*NY Daily News*. "…unpretentious good feelings…bubble through West's loving and humorous play…" –*Star-Ledger*. "…one of the wisest plays I've seen in ages…[from] a master playwright." –*USA Today*. [5W] ISBN: 0-8222-1809-7

★ **THIEF RIVER by Lee Blessing.** Love between two men over decades is explored in this incisive portrait of coming to terms with who you are. "Mr. Blessing unspools the plot ingeniously, skipping back and forth in time as the details require…an absorbing evening." –*NY Times*. "…wistful and sweet-spirited…" –*Variety*. [6M] ISBN: 0-8222-1839-9

★ **THE BEGINNING OF AUGUST by Tom Donaghy.** When Jackie's wife abruptly and mysteriously leaves him and their infant daughter, a pungently comic reevaluation of suburban life ensues. "Donaghy holds a cracked mirror up to the contemporary American family, anatomizing its frailties and miscommunications in fractured language that can be both funny and poignant." –*The Philadelphia Inquirer*. "…[A] sharp, eccentric new comedy. Pungently funny…fresh and precise…" –*LA Times*. [3M, 2W] ISBN: 0-8222-1786-4

★ **OUTSTANDING MEN'S MONOLOGUES 2001–2002 and OUTSTANDING WOMEN'S MONOLOGUES 2001–2002 edited by Craig Pospisil.** Drawn exclusively from Dramatists Play Service publications, these collections for actors feature over fifty monologues each and include an enormous range of voices, subject matter and characters. MEN'S ISBN: 0-8222-1821-6 WOMEN'S ISBN: 0-8222-1822-4

DRAMATISTS PLAY SERVICE, INC.
440 Park Avenue South, New York, NY 10016 212-683-8960 Fax 212-213-1539
postmaster@dramatists.com www.dramatists.com

NEW PLAYS

★ **A LESSON BEFORE DYING by Romulus Linney, based on the novel by Ernest J. Gaines.** An innocent young man is condemned to death in backwoods Louisiana and must learn to die with dignity. "The story's wrenching power lies not in its outrage but in the almost inexplicable grace the characters must muster as their only resistance to being treated like lesser beings." –*The New Yorker.* "Irresistable momentum and a cathartic explosion...a powerful inevitability." –*NY Times.* [5M, 2W] ISBN: 0-8222-1785-6

★ **BOOM TOWN by Jeff Daniels.** A searing drama mixing small-town love, politics and the consequences of betrayal. "...a brutally honest, contemporary foray into classic themes, exploring what moves people to lie, cheat, love and dream. By BOOM TOWN's climactic end there are no secrets, only bare truth." –*Oakland Press.* "...some of the most electrifying writing Daniels has ever done..." –*Ann Arbor News.* [2M, 1W] ISBN: 0-8222-1760-0

★ **INCORRUPTIBLE by Michael Hollinger.** When a motley order of medieval monks learns their patron saint no longer works miracles, a larcenous, one-eyed minstrel shows them an outrageous new way to pay old debts. "A lightning-fast farce, rich in both verbal and physical humor." –*American Theatre.* "Everything fits snugly in this funny, endearing black comedy...an artful blend of the mock-formal and the anachronistically breezy...A piece of remarkably dexterous craftsmanship." –*Philadelphia Inquirer.* "A farcical romp, scintillating and irreverent." –*Philadelphia Weekly.* [5M, 3W] ISBN: 0-8222-1787-2

★ **CELLINI by John Patrick Shanley.** Chronicles the life of the original "Renaissance Man," Benvenuto Cellini, the sixteenth-century Italian sculptor and man-about-town. Adapted from the autobiography of Benvenuto Cellini, translated by J. Addington Symonds. "[Shanley] has created a convincing Cellini, not neglecting his dark side, and a trim, vigorous, fast-moving show." –*BackStage.* "Very entertaining...With brave purpose, the narrative undermines chronology before untangling it...touching and funny..." –*NY Times.* [7M, 2W (doubling)] ISBN: 0-8222-1808-9

★ **PRAYING FOR RAIN by Robert Vaughan.** Examines a burst of fatal violence and its aftermath in a suburban high school. "Thought provoking and compelling." –*Denver Post.* "Vaughan's powerful drama offers hope and possibilities." –*Theatre.com.* "[The play] doesn't put forth compact, tidy answers to the problem of youth violence. What it does offer is a compelling exploration of the forces that influence an individual's choices, and of the proverbial lifelines—be they familial, communal, religious or political—that tragically slacken when society gives in to apathy, fear and self-doubt..." –*Westword.* "...a symphony of anger..." –*Gazette Telegraph.* [4M, 3W] ISBN: 0-8222-1807-0

★ **GOD'S MAN IN TEXAS by David Rambo.** When a young pastor takes over one of the most prestigious Baptist churches from a rip-roaring old preacher-entrepreneur, all hell breaks loose. "...the pick of the litter of all the works at the Humana Festival..." –*Providence Journal.* "...a wealth of both drama and comedy in the struggle for power..." –*LA Times.* "...the first act is so funny...deepens in the second act into a sobering portrait of fear, hope and self-delusion..." –*Columbus Dispatch.* [3M] ISBN: 0-8222-1801-1

★ **JESUS HOPPED THE 'A' TRAIN by Stephen Adly Guirgis.** A probing, intense portrait of lives behind bars at Rikers Island. "...fire-breathing...whenever it appears that JESUS is settling into familiar territory, it slides right beneath expectations into another, fresher direction. It has the courage of its intellectual restlessness...[JESUS HOPPED THE 'A' TRAIN] has been written in flame." –*NY Times.* [4M, 1W] ISBN: 0-8222-1799-6

DRAMATISTS PLAY SERVICE, INC.
440 Park Avenue South, New York, NY 10016 212-683-8960 Fax 212-213-1539
postmaster@dramatists.com www.dramatists.com

NEW PLAYS

★ **THE CIDER HOUSE RULES, PARTS 1 & 2 by Peter Parnell, adapted from the novel by John Irving.** Spanning eight decades of American life, this adaptation from the Irving novel tells the story of Dr. Wilbur Larch, founder of the St. Cloud's, Maine orphanage and hospital, and of the complex father-son relationship he develops with the young orphan Homer Wells. "…luxurious digressions, confident pacing…an enterprise of scope and vigor…" –*NY Times.* "…The fact that I can't wait to see Part 2 only begins to suggest just how good it is…" –*NY Daily News.* "…engrossing…an odyssey that has only one major shortcoming: It comes to an end." –*Seattle Times.* "…outstanding…captures the humor, the humility…of Irving's 588-page novel…" –*Seattle Post-Intelligencer.* [9M, 10W, doubling, flexible casting] PART 1 ISBN: 0-8222-1725-2 PART 2 ISBN: 0-8222-1726-0

★ **TEN UNKNOWNS by Jon Robin Baitz.** An iconoclastic American painter in his seventies has his life turned upside down by an art dealer and his ex-boyfriend. "…breadth and complexity…a sweet and delicate harmony rises from the four cast members…Mr. Baitz is without peer among his contemporaries in creating dialogue that spontaneously conveys a character's social context and moral limitations…" –*NY Times.* "…darkly funny, brilliantly desperate comedy…TEN UNKNOWNS vibrates with vital voices." –*NY Post.* [3M, 1W] ISBN: 0-8222-1826-7

★ **BOOK OF DAYS by Lanford Wilson.** A small-town actress playing St. Joan struggles to expose a murder. "…[Wilson's] best work since *Fifth of July*…An intriguing, prismatic and thoroughly engrossing depiction of contemporary small-town life with a murder mystery at its core…a splendid evening of theater…" –*Variety.* "…fascinating…a densely populated, unpredictable little world." –*St. Louis Post-Dispatch.* [6M, 5W] ISBN: 0-8222-1767-8

★ **THE SYRINGA TREE by Pamela Gien.** Winner of the 2001 Obie Award. A breathtakingly beautiful tale of growing up white in apartheid South Africa. "Instantly engaging, exotic, complex, deeply shocking…a thoroughly persuasive transport to a time and a place…stun[s] with the power of a gut punch…" –*NY Times.* "Astonishing…affecting …[with] a dramatic and heartbreaking conclusion…A deceptive sweet simplicity haunts THE SYRINGA TREE…" –*A.P.* [1W (or flexible cast)] ISBN: 0-8222-1792-9

★ **COYOTE ON A FENCE by Bruce Graham.** An emotionally riveting look at capital punishment. "The language is as precise as it is profane, provoking both troubling thought and the occasional cheerful laugh…will change you a little before it lets go of you." –*Cincinnati CityBeat.* "…excellent theater in every way…" –*Philadelphia City Paper.* [3M, 1W] ISBN: 0-8222-1738-4

★ **THE PLAY ABOUT THE BABY by Edward Albee.** Concerns a young couple who have just had a baby and the strange turn of events that transpire when they are visited by an older man and woman. "An invaluable self-portrait of sorts from one of the few genuinely great living American dramatists…rockets into that special corner of theater heaven where words shoot off like fireworks into dazzling patterns and hues." –*NY Times.* "An exhilarating, wicked…emotional terrorism." –*NY Newsday.* [2M, 2W] ISBN: 0-8222-1814-3

★ **FORCE CONTINUUM by Kia Corthron.** Tensions among black and white police officers and the neighborhoods they serve form the backdrop of this discomfiting look at life in the inner city. "The creator of this intense…new play is a singular voice among American playwrights…exceptionally eloquent…" –*NY Times.* "…a rich subject and a wise attitude." –*NY Post.* [6M, 2W, 1 boy] ISBN: 0-8222-1817-8

DRAMATISTS PLAY SERVICE, INC.
440 Park Avenue South, New York, NY 10016 212-683-8960 Fax 212-213-1539
postmaster@dramatists.com www.dramatists.com